The Wrath of Eve

By

Sharmaine S

ISBN: 9798352004371

Chapter 1
Eve

This is stupid. I'm standing in the toilet cubicle with my hands on my hips in a superman pose. I heard it helps by giving you adrenaline or something like that. I must get this job, so I'm willing to do anything.

It's been a minute; I think it's enough. I open the door and walk out of the cubicle. A dollop of soap and a quick rinse under the tap.

A smartly dressed woman greets me and shows me where to sit. I sit down and wait. My interview is in fifteen minutes, but I'm always early because I'm organised, and I dislike tardiness.

Ten minutes later, I'm seeing other candidates starting to pile in. They sit down at the chairs and exchange smiles. They start talking to each other, there's four of them. One of them looks at me and smiles. I don't return her smile. We're all here for the same job, so I won't waste time befriending my competitors.

Two more candidates walk in: a man and a woman. They both sit next to me. The man smiles and gives me a nod, but I'm not interested. I'm not here for friendship, I'm here for a job. One that I have been preparing for, for a while.

I get called in third, not how I would like but it'll do. I'd rather be interviewed first, set the bar high. I walk into the office with my head up high; posture is important.

"Morning, Mr Kasi," I say stretching my hand out. He places his hand into mine and I firmly shake it. He gestures for me to sit down.

"Miss Gutu, what can you offer me?" He gets straight to the point.

"Sir?"

"I have already seen your C.V. I know where you've worked and your qualifications. What I want to know is why I should hire you?" He looks bored. No wonder the previous interviews were short. He wasn't asking a lot of questions as all the employers usually do.

"What is it that you want?" I could waste time telling him how hard working I am and all that, but it's so cliché. He doesn't seem like the person to be impressed by cliches and mediocrity.

"Someone that can do their job." He looks irritated. I try not to get distracted by his shiny bald head.

"You want to work with Kobe Healthcare."

Mr Kasi raises an eyebrow. That's right, I know that he desperately wants to work with Kobe Healthcare, and frankly, I don't blame him. Kobe Healthcare has many private hospitals in the UK.

"I can help you."

He squints his eyes. "How so?" he asks.

"I'll help you get a meeting with Henry Kobe."

"I can do that myself."

"I will help you come up with an enticing deal. I can help you get a contract with him and other companies."

"You sound sure of yourself." He doubts my abilities.

"I am."

He laughs sarcastically. He leans back in his chair and sets his eyes on me as he strokes his neat circle beard. He looks fascinated. I'm getting to him. I've got to convince him. I need to get this job. I can do this, hook, line and sinker.

"I don't expect you believe me," I say. He raises an eyebrow.

"You can take me on for two months and then decide."

"Two months is a long time and a waste of money if I'm not going to keep you."

I'm not surprised by how direct he is. I anticipated it. I did my research on this man before coming to the interview. I followed him for months, years. I knew his every move. He's been changing assistants like socks over the past year.

"One month," I say.

"Why do you want to work here? For me?"

"Kasi Implants is a reputable company which produces quality products. This company is only going grow and I want to be a part of it. I want to be there when you go international."

Hook.

"You think we'll go international?"

I nod. "I know you will."

"What makes you so sure?"

"The quality of your products, and the growth the company has seen over the past few years"

He's silent for a moment. "Thank you for coming. HR will be in touch with a decision."

"Thank you for having me. I look forward to hearing from them." I maintain eye contact as I shake his hand. He holds my eye contact with a softer expression than when I first walked in.

Line.

As I walk towards the lifts, they open and two people walk out. The man is tall and dressed in fine threads. He's holding a smartphone in his hand. No doubt he's texting something inappropriate to someone's daughter. He's been in the middle of a few scandals in the past year.

The woman is wearing designer threads also, and 28inch wig. It swings as she walks. I never understood how women deal with so much hair. I'm fine with my pixie cut. Doesn't take up time styling in the mornings.

They barely look at me as they walk past me. They're so conceited; Edward and Stephanie Kasi. John Kasi's two eldest. Troublemakers.

I'm home within half an hour. The tubes weren't too full. I take my shoes off and put them on the shoe rack and slip into my house slippers. I get a tub of ice-cream out of the freezer and throw myself on the sofa and switch on the tele.

Becky arrives around 5pm. She finds me chilling on the sofa. "How was your interview?" She asks.

"Fine. How was your day?" I ask.

"Busy."

"I've ordered pizza."

"I guess I can pig out today." She throws herself on the sofa next to me. My mobile vibrates on the coffee table. Unknown number, I raise an eyebrow.

"Hello?" I answer. Better not be telemarketing or some shit like that.

"Good afternoon, my name is Sarah and I'm calling from Kasi Implants. May I speak to Ms Gutu," says the caller in cheerful voice.

"This is her speaking." I sit up.

"Hello there. I'm calling as a follow-up from your interview earlier."

"Yes."

"Mr Kasi would like to offer you the position as his assistant for an initial contractual period of one month."

"That's wonderful, thank you so much."

"We'll see you on Monday. I'll email you some documents including some company regulations and policies."

"That'll be great."

"Okay, enjoy the rest of your week."

"Bye," I smile to myself.

"Was that-

"I got the job!" I yelp.

"Yay!" She screams as she leaps from her seat and wraps her arms around me.

"I'm going to need a favour, though."

"What is it?"

"A meeting with your boss."

"Eh?" She raises an eyebrow.

"I must meet with him."

"Henry is a busy man; I can't just ask him to meet you. Why do you want to meet him anyway?"

"For business reasons. Just let me know when he's free, and I can just *run* into him."

Becky sighs. "I don't what you're up to, but I'll check his schedule and see when you can *run* into him."

That's all I need, just five minutes of Henry Kobe's time.

"Thanks Becky."

Sinker.

Chapter 2
Henry

I rip my off disposable surgical gown and chuck it in the bin. A healthcare assistant is standing close by, tidying up the instruments.

"Be quick!" Michelle: the nurse in charge snaps at her. This is the one thing I never liked in theatres. No one gives the healthcare assistant the respect they deserve because they're at the lowest band. But I notice how hard they work.

"I think she's doing just fine," I say to Michelle.

"Oh, we just need to finish," she smiles awkwardly. That one, she's quite pretentious and is always batting her eyelids at me. I don't operate much anymore but whenever I do, she always finds her way into my theatre. I don't who does the rota, but they must owe her something because she is always scheduled on my cases.

"What's your name?" I ask the healthcare assistant.

"Me?" her eyes fly wide open. I nod. "Martha," she says in almost a whisper.

"How long have you worked here?"

"Three months, sir."

"Call me Henry."

"Eh, okay."

"You're doing a good job." I smile at her and turn on my heel. To me it's important to have good rapport with my staff regardless of their position.

"When are you coming back?" Michelle interjects.

"I don't know," I reply.

"We like having you," Maria; another nurse calls out.

"Thank you all for your hard work." I smile as I head out of the theatre. I really do appreciate their hard work. A surgeon can't do his job without the nurses, healthcare assistants, pathologists, anaesthetists of anyone else. It's all teamwork.

I leave the theatre and go to the changing rooms. I change out of my scrubs and into a white shirt and grey trousers. I check the time; 13.30. I only had two knee replacements, which don't take me that long. I'd have preferred a fuller list, since I don't operate often anymore.

I decide on returning to my office for the rest of the day. The nurses greet me as I walk past them, making my way to the lifts. A woman joins me on the next level. She stands next to me and doesn't press anything.

"Which floor?" I ask her. She turns to face me.

"It's already pressed," she says.

"Oh?"

She's going to the 7th floor, same as me. That floor is only for me and other hospital directors and executives. I have never seen her before. I wonder if she has a meeting with someone.

"Mr Kobe," she extends her hand. I extend mine warily and she shake hers. "Eve Gutu," she says.

"Ms Gutu,"

"It's a pleasure to meet you."

"Thank you." I guess she's here for me. She's dressed in a navy pant suit and a white shirt. She's dressed smartly, so she couldn't be a groupie, as my sister Faith calls them. However, I know I don't have a meeting since it's my day to operate. So, who is she and why is she here?

"I am John Kasi's PA," she says. The doors open and she follows me out.

"I see."

"Kasi Implants is one of the fastest growing orthopaedic implant companies in the U.K."

"I'm aware of them." I keep walking towards my office.

"Great, how about using them as one of your suppliers?"

She's bold. Going straight to the point. Becky springs up to her feet as I approach her desk.

"Good afternoon," she greets me. I nod in response. "Messages." She hands me a small piece of paper. I head into my office and Eve follows me in.

"We have suppliers already," I reply. I lean on the edge of the desk and slip my hands into my pocket.

"There's no harm in trying out new suppliers," she replies. She's tall, slim, small but noticeable hips, and small breasts.

"Our hospital is supplied by international companies with quality products. I have no reason to try and change that now."

"Your suppliers are from Germany and Sweden. Kasi Implants is one of the only British implants companies. Though it's not massive, it has impressive products. Why not work with a British brand?"

She's well spoken, and very direct.

"Did John ask you to ambush me? You could've called my PA to schedule a meeting."

"I could've but there was no guarantee that I'd be able to schedule one."

"So, ambushing me was the better option?"

"Yes." She's unapologetic and now I'm intrigued by her.

"I'm not interested."

"Won't you at least have a look at the implants?"

"No."

"Can I still set up an appointment with your PA? I think Mr Kasi would do a better job of convincing you."

I stare at her blankly for a moment, and she holds my stare. She seems like a woman that doesn't give up easily.

"I've got work to do," I say as I walk around the desk and settle into my seat.

"Okay, I'll leave you to it. See you tomorrow," she says. I notice that she has nice lips.

"Excuse me?"

"I'm going to keep ambushing you until you agree to a meeting."

I open my mouth to speak but she cuts me off.

"I know you're busy. The meeting doesn't have to be a long one. Five minutes is enough," she turns on her heel and marches out of the office. She's a beautiful woman with a manly walk.

She's piqued my interest.

Chapter 3

Eve

Thanks to Becky, I know that Henry drinks green tea every morning. I don't understand why, coffee is life.

I wait at the entrance of the hospital with a green tea for him. An expensive bloody green tea because it's just by Harley Street. It's cold and early but it's worth it if I can run into Henry. He'll probably think I'm a stalker, but I have to set a meeting between him and John.

It's 7am when Henry arrives. I watch him walk towards me. I've seen pictures of him but he's different in person. Tall, dark chocolate skin, a full beard that actually connects.

"Morning," I say to Henry. "Tea?"

"You actually came back?" he takes the tea from me and takes a sip. "Green tea?" he looks surprised.

"Yes. Have you reconsidered?"

"Straight to the point."

"That's the kind of woman I am. I don't beat around the bush."

"Mhmm."

"We only need five minutes of your time." I follow him into the building. He smells nice.

"What's the point If I'm not going to change suppliers?"

"Just a meeting, that's all I'm asking for." That's all I need. I just need to show John how capable I am. I've got one month to impress him.

We stop at the lifts. Henry looks at me as he drinks his tea. It's no wonder he's in good shape, he drinks green tea$ and according to Becky, he goes to the gym quite often. I try not let my eyes wonder to his muscular arms.

"Will you show up here tomorrow?" he asks me. There's a glimmer of mischief in his eyes. I hope he's not challenging me because I will accept but I won't be pleased. I hate begging anyone. This man must just agree to a meeting and set me free.

"Yes, if I have to," I reply.

"Are you that determined?"

I nod. "Kasi implants has been trying to work with you for years."

"John has never been this persistent. Why are you only coming to me now?"

"Because I've only just started working for him and this is the first thing I wish to achieve."

His eyebrows slowly rise and gives me a cheeky look, I don't know what that's all about.

"Your hospitals are the best in the country. I can see why Mr Kasi is desperate to work with you. I want this deal for him because it's good for my career progression."

"You're straightforward, and you know what you want."

"Yes. I don't like to beat around the bush or pussyfoot."

Pussyfoot is probably not a professional word, but it's too late to take it back now. I hold his gaze for a moment. There is silence between us; it's tense. His hazel eyes are piercing as if he can see into my soul. Wording...

"Call my PA," he says at last. His voice is deep.

"You're agreeing to a meeting?" I'm surprised.

"Five minutes."

The lift doors open, and he walks in. I nod.

"Thank you," I say. I turn and walk off.

**

I arrive early on Monday morning, of course, because I hate tardiness. It's my first day, and I must make a good impression. I see John walking out of his office and towards the lifts.

"Good morning," I say to him.

"Come with me," he says. I haven't even left the lift. I nod and stay in there. He walks in and presses the G button. "I need you to come with me to a meeting," he says.

"Okay." I didn't expect to be attending any meetings with him just yet. I like it, being thrown into the deep end. I always hated jobs that start with tedious induction weeks with lots of reading.

We get into his car, a Rolls Royce with beige leather seats. I've never been in one, and I'm not surprised that John has such an expensive car. He is a wealthy man, and his family is renowned for being flashy. We sit in the back since he's got a driver.

"You sit quietly and observe," he starts giving me instructions. Most of what he says is common sense. I nod as he speaks. "I hope you're taking note of what I'm saying. I don't like repeating myself," he adds.

"Yes, Mr Kasi." I get it. I don't like repeating myself either.

We arrive at our destination about half an hour later. It would've been quicker if we had taken the tube, but wealthy people don't ride the tube. They'd rather sit in their expensive cars in traffic and pay congestion charges than take the dirty tube.

We're welcomed by a receptionist and then ushered to a conference room. There are some people in the conference room already. John exchanges greetings ~~with them~~ before he joins them at the table. I take my place next to him.

They begin discussing their current contract. I'm sitting there taking notes and absorbing as much information as I can. The meeting is finished not too long after. John and I leave and head back to his car. *shortly*

As we climb in, I get an alert on my phone. I look at it, and Ed Kasi is the reason for the alert. I have alerts for the whole family on social networks and news outlets. I keep tabs on them.

"Mr Kasi, Ed seems to be in a bit of a situation," I Say.

"What kind of a situation?" he sounds so fed up.

"I'm not sure of the details or how bad it is, but it's all-over social media."

"He's probably at the wretched studio of his." John sighs and then instructs the driver to take us to his son's studio in Soho. We arrive in less than half an hour.

John jumps out of the car and rushes into one of the buildings. I follow behind, and we walk into Ed's art studio. ~~He has a studio in Soho where he spends a lot of his time.~~

We walk right into a chaotic scene. Ed is naked with his hands covering his manhood, and behind him is a woman with a long blonde weave. She is wrapped in a bed sheet. There's another woman fully dressed, raging with a knife in her hand. I guess she was the one who posted the naked picture of Ed online.

"What the hell is going on in here?" John spits out.

"Dad?" Ed's eyebrows shoot up as his head whips in our direction.

"Your son is a liar and a cheater!" the raging woman cries out. I look at her from head to toe. She's beautiful, but I've never seen her with Ed in any pictures.

"Babe, it's not what it looks like," Ed. I narrow my gaze at him. That's the lamest thing people say. It's always what it looks like!

"I'm not an idiot!" Babe screams back.

With the knife in her hand, I back to differ.

"What are you doing?"

She's pointing the knife at her own neck. "I'm tired of this shit!" she says, tears streaming down her face. I roll my eyes. She wants to kill herself because of a man? Bruh.

"Oh God," John rubs his eyebrows.

"Don't come closer!" she screams when Ed tries to approach her. He stops when she presses the knife against her olive skin. She whips her wig off and chucks it on the floor. I gasp. Why take the wig off? Her cornrows aren't even neat.

"Temi, I'm sorry," says Ed.

"No, you're not. I'm tired of you treating me like this," Temi responds and presses the knife even more. Blood starts coming out. The blonde one starts screaming.

"Oh, shut up," I say to the blonde one. I can't stand here any longer and witness this madness.

"Excuse me?" She looks at me as if she's about to fight me.

"Who are you?" Ed asks me.

"Temi, look at me," I say. She doesn't immediately do as I say. I have to repeat myself, which I hate doing. She looks at me, tears streaming down her face and her hand shaking. "You're a beautiful woman," I say.

"Who the fuck are you?" She asks.

"Please don't hurt yourself over a man."

"I beg you get out of my face, bruv."

I sigh. I have to stop with my professional tone for her to take me seriously. "Listen, yeah, this guy is a waste, man. Like wagwan? Why are you degrading yourself over a man that treats you like fucking shit?" I yelp. Everyone looks at me as if I'm strange, except John. He looks amused.

word?.

"Temi put the fuckin knife down and act like you've got some sense init," I continue.

"Listen, yeah-

"No, you listen," I cut her off. "You can do better than him. Move on, bruv, this shit is embarrassing!"

"Who the fuck are you?" Ed sounds irritated. I wave him off my hand. I approach Temi and snatch the knife from her. Probably not how you should act in such a situation, but I don't have the skills to deescalate such situations. I'm impatient, and I hate seeing black women degrade themselves over men.

Temi looks startled. I take a deep breath before I say anything. Becky always told me that I need to be a bit softer with people. "Please leave and forget about this entire thing," There's damage control to do also. We can't have the media getting a hold of this entire situation.

"How can I do that?" She asks.

"He's not worth it. There's plenty of fish in the sea," I hate that saying, but that's what people always say when advising you to move on.

"I guess," She replies.

"Men show you when they don't want you. There's no use in hanging on. He'll only cheat on you again. So, spare yourself the heartache and move on while you can. And please, let's leave everything that happened today in here."

She nods. "You asshole! You'll never find a woman like me. You hid me from the public and cheated on him. I'm tired of your crap. I guess I really should move on. Don't come begging me to take you back. I'm done!" she says to Ed. I doubt that he would come begging her, but if he did, she probably would get back with him. Temi turns on her heels and heads for the door.

"Your wig," I point out. She walks back, embarrassed and picks up her wig and scampers out of the room. John is watching me, amused. Ed looks annoyed. "You created this mess," I say to him. I don't know why he's annoyed, though.

"Who the hell are you?" he asks me.

"My new PA," says John.

Not a temporary one either; I know I'm staying past a month now.

incorrect use of ;
missing words
wording - too many
        - repetitive
dialogue - too much!

Chapter 4
Eve

What a first day, I'm having.

"Get dressed; we're leaving," John instructs his son.

"Dad-

off limits

Closed

"This art studio," he waves his finger around. "Is now shut until further notice."

"What?" Ed chuckles sarcastically.

"Fine. I will just have to cut you off."

Rich people's problems. I've always had to work for everything I had. No one could ever cut me off.

"But dad," he whines.

"Meet me in the car in five minutes." John turns on his heel and walks out of the room.

I look at the blonde one. "Get dressed and get the hell out. Don't speak a word about any of this to anyone. I don't want to read about it online or in the newspaper." I follow John and leave the love birds to get dressed.

Being a PA to a wealthy person means handling their image as well. If Ed has any more scandals, this could affect the family's image and, ultimately, the company. The value of shares will plunge, and investors will pull out.

I can't have the company's image to plummet, not yet. I need to be irreplaceable and valuable to John if my plan is to work.

Ed and the blonde one are out within minutes. He gives her money, and then she's off. I frown. I can tell there's nothing deep going on between them, and yet he's giving her money. She's probably with him for the money.

I sit in the front with the driver, and Ed sits in the back with his father. As we drive back to the office, John tells his son that he needs to be more focused within the company. He can't just be working there when he feels like it. If he wants to take over from his father, then he needs to prove himself. He's a spoilt brat that needs to grow up and take responsibility for his actions.

I agree with everything John is saying, but I say nothing. Ed needs a slap; and some tough love. Both him and Stephanie, too actually. They're all spoilt and need to learn how to work for the things they have.

We arrive at the office just before lunchtime. John orders his son to go home and clean up.

"This is your desk," John says to me. I look at the wooden desk outside his office. There is a computer and a phone on the desk, a leather chair and filing cabinets behind it. The place looks messy. "Acquaint yourself with the area," he adds. I nod. He goes into his office before I even say anything. My phone rings.

"Becky?" Why is she calling me during working hours?

"Eve," She answers.

"What's up?"

"I have checked Mr Kobe's diary, and I can squeeze you in for an appointment soon."

"Yes!" I search the messy desk for an appointment diary to no avail. I grab a piece of paper and pen. "When?"

"16th, 10 am."

"16th of what?"

"October." Her tone suggests I should've known which month she was on about.

"That's next week?"

"Take it or leave it. He doesn't have any other openings for months."

"Damn, okay." If John is busy, he'll have to be free because it's the opportunity he's been waiting for, for years.

"Already making personal phone calls during work."

I turn and see John leaning against the door frame looking at me. His thick eyebrows are knit together.

"Thank you, Becky, we'll take that appointment; goodbye." I hang up. "That was Henry Kobe's secretary," I say to John.

"What?" his eyebrows shoot up.

"We have an appointment with him next week Monday Morning."

John stares at me with his eyes widened. Any wider, and they'd fall out. He's probably wondering how I got an appointment so quickly. I want to gloat, but I have to remain professional.

"I searched for your appointment diary to check your schedule, but I couldn't find it. So, I just agreed to the appointment. I'll sort out your schedule."

"Okay," he tries to suppress a smile, but I can see that he's impressed and happy. "How?" he asks.

"I have my ways."

He nods and heads back into his office.

Sarah from HR comes by to show me some stuff. The last PA had been fired so abruptly, leaving no time to do a handover. Sarah gives me the company tablet and system passwords. It's a crappy handover, but It's something.

I start by tidying up the desk and rearranging everything. I clean the desk and chair. Then I familiarise myself with the systems and check John's schedule. He has an appointment next Monday morning. I'll rearrange that appointment because this one with Henry Kobe is a golden opportunity, one John can't afford to lose.

I arrive home after Becky. She's already in the kitchen cooking. The house smells heavenly. I take my shoes and coat off.

"Hey," I say to Becky. She looks over her shoulder. Her curly hair is piled atop her head in a messy bun.

"Hi, how was your first day?" she asks.

"Fine."

She looks at me with a frown on her face. "Just fine?"

"We went to a meeting and then to Ed Kasi's studio. The stupid boy had gotten himself into a situation with two women." I roll my eyes. I dislike men that live like that. If you can't commit to one woman, then just don't get into a relationship, simple.

"What happened with Ed?" Becky loves to gossip. I start telling her all about it, and she's laughing so hard.

"I'm hungry; what are you making?"

"Grilled chicken breast, sauteed vegetables and salad."

I narrow my gaze. "No carbs?" I asked.

"No, we're eating healthy, remember?" it's not even like she has weight to lose.

"I don't remember agreeing to this."

"Come on, Eve."

Fucksake. Chicken breast is dry already; now we're eating it with vegetables and no carbs. I might've to start stashing snacks in my room because I can't cope.

Chapter 5
Henry

"Morning, Mr Kobe," Becky says as I approach her desk.

"Hi, Becky. How was your weekend?" I ask her.

"It was fine, thank you. How was yours?"

"No date or anything?"

"No." She laughs and then picks up her tablet. She clears her throat. "You have a meeting with Kasi Implants at 10am," She starts telling me about my day.

"Hmm." I had almost forgotten about my meeting with them. I listen to Becky ramble on.

She stops talking. I nod and go to my office. "You have to get out more," I call over my shoulder as I shut the door. Becky is a good secretary but seems to have a boring life. She's never up to anything over the weekends and barely takes time off. She's twenty-nine, fiver years than me but her social life suggests she's much older *differently*.

It's 9.55 am when Becky buzzes the phone and tells me that John Kasi has arrived. He's early, but I have some paperwork to finish, so he'll have to wait until 10am.

Becky walks John Kasi into my office at 10 sharp. I stand up and extend my hand. "Mr Kasi," I say.

"Please, call me John," He replies gleefully.

"Hello John, call me Henry."

He shakes my hand. Firmly.

My eyes land on my stalker. She's wearing a black pant suit which hugs her curves nicely. Her black shirt is loose, which is not surprising considering her small chest. It does, however, expose her long neck. I follow her neck up to her chiselled jawline and high cheekbones. She's wearing no makeup, but her chestnut brown skin is flawless, and her eyebrows are perfectly shaped.

"Ms Gutu," I greet her.

"Good morning, Mr Kobe," she replies, cooly as an ice cube.

"Henry," I smile, but she doesn't return my smile. She's wearing such a stern look on her face. I wonder if she's always that serious.

We sit down at the glass table on the other side of the room. Becky joins us.

"Thank you for granting us this meeting," says John. I nod.

"You have Ms Gutu to thank for that." My eyes flick to her for a second and then back to John.

John smiles and nods. "I understand that this will be a brief meeting as you are a busy man. So, I will get right to it," he says. I like people that get straight to the point.

John starts speaking about his company and how amazing they are, but he's not telling me why I need them because I don't. I have my own suppliers. I don't need to change anything.

I lean back in my seat and stare at him blankly. He's underwhelming. I check my watch, and two minutes have passed since he started speaking.

"John," I say firmly. "Thank you for coming down here, but I'm not looking for new suppliers."

"May I interject?" My stalker, the ice queen. She leans forward in her seat.

"Sure." I would rather listen to her than John anyway.

"I see that you will be starting a pro-bono clinic next Spring."

"Yes." It's not public information; I'm impressed that she knows about that.

"I think it's a noble thing that you're doing."

"Thank you."

"What if we provide the implants for your surgeries?"

I raise an eyebrow. John looks at her in shock. It seems he's not sure what his PA is capable of.

"Just because the surgeries are pro-bono does not mean that I'll use just any implants."

"Kasi Implants aren't just any implants."

"I have standards." I lean forward in my seat and meet her brown eyes.

"We can meet them."

"Yes, we can," John interjects. I ignore him and keep my gaze on Eve.

"Kasi implants are made of ceramic. They're durable and reliable. Only 10% of our patients have had revisions within ten years from the initial replacement."

"Okay." I'm intrigued.

"Our implants are reliable. I understand your concerns. There is enough time between now and the clinic's opening for you to fully inspect our products. You can visit our labs, look at our reports, and test out the products before using them on patients. If you're not satisfied by spring next year, we won't proceed with our contract."

The way she's coming at me, you would think that it's her company. I stare at her as I contemplate my answer. She holds my stare, barely blinking. Icy.

"We're prepared to offer a 10% discount for the first few months of the contract," Says John.

"Okay, Becky will be in touch to set up future meetings. I will need to inspect every aspect of the implants before I decide."

"Alright. Thank you for your time. We won't let you down." John shakes my hand. He seems proud, as if he changed my mind, but the ice queen did all the leg work.

I shake her hand. Surprisingly, it's cold. But it's soft. She gives a firm handshake.

"Thank you for your time," she says to me. Her tone is cool, like her hands.

"See you soon," I reply with a small smile.

**

"Hey," she approaches the table with a smile. She's dressed up as usual. She knows what to wear to accentuate her body.

"Hello gorgeous," I reply, pulling out her chair.

"Thank you." She giggles.

I sit across her. She flips her long weave back. She's wearing a low-cut white dress revealing her cleavage. No doubt she's wearing a push-up bra.

She tells me about her day as we eat. It's only our third date, but I already know this isn't going anywhere. There's no substance in her conversations, but she's gorgeous. She's into me, and I'm trying to give her a chance. I don't want to be rash with my decisions.

We're standing in front of her house around 10pm. I snake my arm around her waist and pull her closer to me.

"Oooh," she giggles. I run my hand down her back and caress her bottom. "Henry," she whispers my name in my ear. I'm looking at her; she's running her hands down my chest.

"Hmm." I didn't expect her to be so bold. She's holding my package in her hands.

"Big." She smiles. "Why don't you come in?"

Fucksake.

"Your parents are home." That's not the issue here. The ice queen's face is suddenly on my mind.

"You won't see them; they're probably sleeping. We can get in through the back." She plants a kiss on my neck. I lean in and kiss her on the cheek.

"Next time, Steph,"

Chapter 6
Eve

"Girls, wake up!"

My eyes fly wide open. That voice is familiar.

"It's already 9am! You should be up already!"

Lord have mercy. I sit up. What is she doing here? I drag myself out of bed and head to the living room. I stand in the doorway, glaring at her. I love her, but for goodness sake, it's Saturday!

"Eve!" she places her hands on her waist.

"Gogo," I'm still rubbing my eyes.

"Where's the other one? Rebecca!" She shouts.

"Gogo!" she comes out of her room running. Poor bird, it's not her grandmother, but she's subjected to the same treatment as me.

"Two beautiful young women sleeping in so late like this," says Gogo. Becky and I look at each other. "What are you looking at each other for?" she approaches me and hugs me. I love her embrace, the only person I bother hugging. She hugs Becky also.

"How are you, gogo?" Becky.

"I'm fine, my dear. Now go wash your faces and get ready for spring cleaning, both of you."

"Eh?" I'm not happy about this.

"Now."

I drag my feet to the bathroom. "It's your fault for offering her a key," I say to Becky in the bathroom.

"You think not having a key would stop her?" She asks.

"No." She would probably bang on the door until we open for her.

We're done in a few seconds. We got to meet my grandmother in the living room. We're put to work within seconds. I am clean and tidy like she raised me, but you know how it is with adults. Your cleaning is never good enough.

Gogo puts on her gospel playlist while we clean. She starts singing. It's just like old times. I love her, but I would rather be sleeping.

We finish around 11 am. Gogo even made us clean our rooms and then inspected our work. At least mine is usually clean. Becky's one looks like a bombsite. Gogo wasn't impressed. How can a beautiful woman sleep in such a state? Gogo asked. Gogo cooks while we shower and get changed.
She
"Mr Kobe was impressed by you," Becky says, walking into my room without knocking as usual. It's not strange that we're almost thirty years old and housemates. It's Hammersmith, London zone 2, house prices are ridiculous. So, we rent together while saving for house deposits.

"I'm not surprised," I say. It's been five days since John and I had a meeting with Henry Kobe. John was surprised and impressed by me. He's a man of few words, but I could see it in his face. He will be keeping me on after a month.

"We'll need to sort out our boss's diaries."

I nod. "What is it like working for him? What's he like?" I'm a little bit curious about this man we're about to go in business with. I know what they say about him in the tabloids; shrewd businessman. An orthopaedic consultant who is in line to be the CEO of Kobe healthcare.

"He's a nice man, very kind boss. I like working for him." Becky shrugs.

"Let's not talk about work today." I spring up to my feet. "Let's go eat."

Gogo is dishing the food as we walk into the kitchen. She set up the table nicely. I smile; real food. She doesn't make salads and greens like Becky has been doing lately. There's rice, beans, kale, oxtail. I'm excited.

We wash our hands before sitting at the table. Gogo says grace, and then we start eating.

"Why are you both still single?" Gogo asks.

Here we go again.

"I just haven't met the right man yet," Becky replies.

"How will you know when you meet the right man if you never date anyone." Gogo looks at Becky as she eats.

"It's hard to find the good guys these days."

Gogo narrows her gaze at Becky. "You just have no game."

I burst into laughter. There's no way gogo just said game. What does she know about game? Who's been teaching her slang?

"What are you laughing at? You've been single since 1980."

"Bruh," My jaw drops. Savage. I wasn't even born in 1980. Becky laughs at me. "Gogo, you're not dating either."

"Says who?"

What the fuck? I'd said that as a joke.

"Gogo," Becky gasps. I've stopped eating. I'm staring at her waiting for an answer.

"You're shook?" Gogo.

No, who's teaching her slang?

"Are you seeing someone?" I ask.

"I am a woman, you know."

I frown. She better not say I have needs.

"An attractive one at that." She carries on eating. I'm still staring at her, waiting for an explanation. "His name is Ernest."

Lord Jesus, take the wheel!

"Ernest," Becky smiles.

"He's a lovely man." Gogo is now smiling.

I love my oxtail, but I need to get to the bottom of this story. I put my fork down.

"Whom you met where?" I ask.

"Church."

I should've guessed.

"Church, that's where it's at." Becky is enjoying this far too much.

"It was at a fundraiser for a charity." She giggles. "Ernest came to my stall to buy some of my baked treats. Since then, he can't get enough of my cookie."

Becky almost spits out drink as she laughs.

"Cookies, gogo, cookies." I feel sick.

"What?" she looks confused.

"How long have you been seeing this man?"

"Five months."

"You've been seeing someone for five months and never told me."

us

"I don't need to tell you my business."

Ha! But if it was me saying that.

"Okay." I've heard enough. Let me <u>reconcile</u> with my food. I pick up my fork and start eating.

I didn't expect my day to begin like this. My seventy-year-old grandmother has a boyfriend.

I can't.

"How's work?" Gogo asks.

"Work is fine." Becky answers. "This one got a new job." She points at me with her fork. I want to smack her with it.

"Why didn't you tell me?" She looks at me with her eyebrows furrowed.

Because of whom I'm working for.

"It's nothing gogo. I'm a PA for someone in the health sector."

"In the NHS?"

"No, private. Anyway, let's not talk about work. Let's eat." I gulp my juice. I can't have her find out that I'm working for John Kasi. She'd skin me alive.

Chapter 7
Henry

"You're late," ma complains as I walk into the dining room. Everyone is already sitting at the table.

"Sorry, ma," I kiss her on the cheek before I take my place at the head of the table opposite my father.

"Son," My father nods.

"Hi, dad."

"Yo," Nate, my brother.

"Yo."

"Why are you late anyway?" Faith, my twenty-two-year-old sister.

"Were you with a woman?" Grace, my twenty-year-old sister, the baby of the family. The two of them are so nosey and talkative. Ma raises an eyebrow at me as she puts a plate of food in front of me.

"Thank you, "I say to her. The roast looks good. It doesn't matter that my parents have staff to cook and clean. Ma always makes sure to cook the Sunday roast for her family every week.

"Answer your sister," she orders.

"This looks good." I pick up my fork and dig in. I don't want to talk about my dating life.

"Henry, I'm not getting any younger. I need grandkids." She takes a sip of her wine. At thirty-four, I think I'm still too young to settle down.

"You're too young and too beautiful to be a grandmother." I wink. My sisters burst into laughter.

"You think you're slick," says Faith.

"Can you even pull?" Grace asks.

"What do you know about pulling?" I frown. She better not be pulling any guys. She's too young.

"I bet I can-

"You can what?" Nate jumps in. He's just as overprotective over the girls as I am. He's also more unpredictable and short-tempered.

"Jeez," she rolls her eyes.

"Are you seeing someone, Henry?" Ma asks. I clear my throat and take a sip of my drink. She stares at me, waiting on my response. She's regal and poise. She's wearing a white elaborate blouse and pearls. Her hair is styled up into a neat updo. You'd think people would dress down during the weekends when chilling with their families. Not my mother. You'll never see her undone.

"Not really," I've never been able to lie to her. No one could. She can see through anyone.

"What does that mean?"

"We've only been on a few dates; it's too early to tell where this is going."

"You're actually seeing someone?" Grace's eyebrows shoot up.

"Don't be naïve. Women throw themselves at him. He has groupies. I'm surprised he's not a player." Faith narrows her gaze at me.

"Bring her over to my birthday party," says Ma. The party that's meant to be a surprise, but she found out about it, just as she finds out about everything. And being the control freak that she is, she's making sure the party is being planned according to her standards.

"Ah, no." I cut into my beef and eat. There's no way I'm bringing Steph to her birthday party. Even though the party is in a month and a half, I doubt that Steph and I will be at the point of meeting each other's families.

"And why is that?"

"Let's stop interrogating him, Esther. Henry will introduce a woman to us when he's ready," My father comes to my rescue. I give him a nod as I take a sip of my drink.

**

"Kasi Implants would like to invite you on a lab tour," Becky says to me.

"Okay, set it up," I reply. It's been a week since I met with John Kasi. It's not a surprise that they're getting in touch so soon.

 "Let me check your schedule." Becky taps the tablet screen.

"Hello?" I hear as the door swings open. Steph walks in with white paper bags in her hands.

"Ms, you can't just walk in here." Becky frowns. "You have to book an appointment first."

"Oops." She looks unapologetic. "I've brought lunch." She waves the bag at me.

"Mr Kobe is a busy-

Steph waves her hand, cutting Becky off. "He's got time for me, don't you, Henry?" She says. I rub my eyebrows. They're both looking at me, waiting for me to speak.

"Steph," I say softly.

"See, he knows me and doesn't mind me being here," Steph says to Becky. She sits down opposite me and puts the paper bag on the table.

"Please excuse us, Becky."

"Get us some water, Becky. Bottled, please, I don't do tap." Steph orders Becky.

"Steph, please don't be rude to Becky."

Just because she is beautiful, it doesn't give her the right to be rude to my staff.

"She works for you."

"Meaning?"

"She's the help. I should be able to ask for anything I need."

Becky's jaw hangs open. I can't believe what Steph just said also. I'm quickly turned off by a stinking attitude.

"Becky, you may leave us," I say. Becky walks out of the office and shuts the door behind her. "That was inappropriate," I say sternly.

"It wasn't that bad." She doesn't seem to understand what she did wrong. That makes it worse. There's no remorse. I guess this will be the end of us.

She fishes out two boxes of sushi out of the paper bag.

"I thought we could have lunch together." She smiles and tucks a lock of hair behind her ear. She's gorgeous. It's a shame that she doesn't have manners, and frankly, she's uninteresting. She hands me chopsticks.

"I only have about ten minutes to spare." I start eating the sushi.

"Only ten?" She looks disappointed.

"You should've called ahead."

She pouts.

"Can I see you after work?" She gives me puppy eyes. Shame I'm unaffected.

"I don't think I can today."

"Why didn't you come in last time you dropped me off home?"

"It's your parents' house. I didn't want to run into your parents at night."

It's partly true; I didn't want to meet her parents after spending the night or about to spend the night.

"Maybe I can come to your house instead." She plays with her long weave.

"Maybe." I give her half a smile. Tempting.

Steph puts her chopsticks down and closes the box. I noticed that she doesn't eat much in my presence.

"Full already?" I ask.

"Yeah. I'm not one of those women that feels the need to overindulge on food."

"Okay…"

She walks around the desk, keeping her eyes on mine. She sits on my lap and flips her hair back.

"What are you doing?"

She presses a small kiss against my lips.

"I have a meeting in a few minutes," I say.

"You can be a little bit late," she whispers in my ear. She runs her hand down my chest, down to my manhood. Just then, the phone rings. I press the button, and Becky reminds me of my meeting.

"Sorry," I say to Steph.

"Fine." She kisses me again and rubs my manhood. "Call me." She springs up to her feet and walks out of the office.

I laugh to myself. Steph is such a bold woman who will go after what she wants. I'm tempted to give it to her, but I don't want to complicate things. I don't see a future between us, it's better to end things now, but she's attractive and tempting.

Chapter 8
Eve

I arrive at the office before Mr Kasi. This could be my chance! I dash into his office with the potted plant I just bought from the florist on my way in. I put the flower on his desk and open the top drawer. There's not much in there, just some stationery. I go through the next two drawers and find nothing incriminating.

The bottom drawer is locked. I raise an eyebrow. Why would it be the only locked drawer, and where is the key?

I notice a cabinet behind the desk; I open it and see a safe mounted inside. I want to take a crack at the safe, but I don't want John to catch me. He often comes early. Just then, I hear the ding of the lift followed by quick footsteps. I quickly shut the cabinet.

"Eve?" John frowns as we lock eyes. He is standing in the doorway with Ed.

"Morning," I say.

"What are you doing?"

"I was bringing in this flower." I move it slightly, pretending to position it on his desk and silently hoping he didn't see me shut the cabinet. "It's eucalyptus. It might help with your headaches."

"Ah," he walks over and sniffs the plant before taking his place behind the desk. "Thank you," he says. Ed slowly walks in, keeping his gaze on me.

"Ed," I say.

"Eve." He responds.

"I need you to take Ed to your meeting," John.

"What?" Ed spits out and looks at his father in disbelief. I, too, look at him, hoping for an explanation.

"I want Ed to be more involved with company matters."

"And the best place to start is by hanging out with *her*?" he sounds disgusted when he says her. I'm not thrilled either about being around him because I know his character. He doesn't know me, what's his problem?

"Yes. Eve has proved herself to be an asset to the company."

"Has she now?" Ed looks at me from head to toe before bursting into a sarcastic chuckle.

"She secured a meeting with Henry Kobe."

"How?" Ed's eyeballs almost fall out.

"A task you failed to complete for many years. That's why I want you to go to meetings with her. You might learn something."

Ed's jaw tightens as he glares at me. Jealousy is stained all over his face. It's not my fault that he spends more time under skirts that doing something #worthwhile with his life. I excuse myself and go to my desk.

It's 11am when I leave for the meeting at a hospital in Brixton. and I'm annoyed that Ed is tagging along.

"We'll get the tube," I say as we walk out of the building.

"The what?" he looks at me as if I've lost my mind.

"It'll be quicker. There's so much traffic right now, and I don't want to be late." I walk off before he says anything else. I don't want to argue with him about this. He curses and then walks after me.

"How far is it to the station? Can't we at least get the car there?"

I narrow my gaze at him and say nothing. He's a typical spoilt kid. He can't even walk for a few minutes.

"What's your deal anyway?" he asks me.

"What?"

"What were you doing in my father's office?"

"Bringing him a plant."

"Why? Trying to become a mistress or something."

"I'm not you."

"What's that supposed to mean?"

"I don't just sleep with anyone."

"You don't know me!"

I ignore him as we walk into the tube. I take out my oyster card.

"I don't have one," he says, looking at my oyster.

"Use your bank card," I say.

"Huh? Really?" he pulls out his wallet. I sigh. He's so out of touch with the typical day to day life.

"As long as it's contactless. Just tap the yellow circle on the baffle gates."

He nods and follows my lead. He cusses every time someone walks into him. He's too slow getting on the tube. I grab his trench coat and pull him on board. The doors shut as soon as he's in. I sigh and hold onto the pole. It's going to be a long day.

"Hold onto the pole," I instruct Ed.

"Ew, no," he says. The tube starts moving, and he almost falls over. I take his hand and put it on the pole by force. The tube gets fuller at the next stop, and Ed doesn't seem happy. He frowns as the crowd squashes him against the door. He looks so out of place with his designer suit and expensive rings.

We're in Brixton about half an hour later, and we get the bus to the hospital. Ed isn't happy about that, but I ignore his protests.

The meeting with the head of orthopaedics at the hospital lasts about half an hour. They want to use Kasi Implants for their knee replacements. The meeting is only a formality; they seem to have made up their minds. The next step is signing the contracts for which John will have to be present.

I'm grateful for a quick finish. I just want to return to the office and be free from this spoilt brat. He's squirted alcohol gel on his hands at least five times since we left Kasi Implants.

"I might catch a taxi back to the office," he says to me.

"If you have money to burn, then be my guest," I reply.

"That meeting was nothing special. I don't see why my father asked me to come with you."

"You're so spoiled."

"Excuse me?"

"You're just complaining and complaining. You want to take over from your father when he retires, but it doesn't seem you know much about the business, and you're just lazy to work for it." too

"Who do you think you are? I let the incident at the studio slide."

"You let it slide?" I snort. "If anything, you should've thanked me for helping you get out of that messy situation. Maybe Temi should've stabbed you. Maybe then you'd come to your senses. Grow up and take responsibility for your actions."

I take off. I don't have time to argue with a spoiled, entitled big kid. child

**

John and I arrive at the lab just before 10am. We don't wait long, and Henry arrives. He is dressed in a crisp white shirt and navy trousers. His fine threads do nothing to hide his muscular physique. His beard looks neatly trimmed.

"Morning, Mr Kobe," John shakes his hand. I notice the expensive watch on Henry's wrist.

"Morning, call me Henry." His deep voice booms in the lobby. He turns his attention towards me. "Ms Gutu." There's something about the way he says my name.

"Mr Kobe," I say. He shakes my hand. His hand is warm and soft. Unlike my cold hands, I'm embarrassed, actually. I want to snatch my hand back, but he's still holding my hand as he gazes into my eyes. Something about his hazel eyes causes my breath to get jammed up in my throat and my heart to race.

What is happening to me?

Chapter 9
Henry

The ice queen with the ice-cold hands. Again, her hand is cold. I want to hold onto it longer and warm her up, but that's inappropriate. She's wearing a pantsuit again, this time a grey one.

"Shall we go in?" John says. I let go of Eve's hand.

"After you," I say to John.

I don't always go to meetings with Becky. I sent her on a different errand. I'm grateful for John bringing Eve.

A technician greets us and provides us with labcoats and googles. She gives us a tour of the lab, answering any questions I have. I'm impressed by what I see. The lab is clean, everything has its position. I take notice of the technicians and how they work. I also get the opportunity to inspect the raw materials.

The tour is finished A after an hour. I barely heard anything from Eve within that hour. She strikes me as the woman who picks her words carefully.

"May I invite you over for lunch on Saturday?" John says to me.

"Lunch?" I'm not keen.

"Yes, at my house. I'm not taking no for an answer."

"I'll have to check my schedule."

"It'll be great to have you ~~there~~. This way we can get a chance to know each other better. Eve will reach out with the details." His phone rings. "I'm sorry, I have to take this." He shakes my hand before he walks off. Eve and I are left alone, standing in the lobby.

"I will reach out to your assistant with details of the lunch," She says. She's soft-spoken, but that doesn't fool me. She seems like a feisty one. I caught a glimpse of it at our last meeting.

"Are you attending this lunch too?"

"Yes."

"Hmm." I'm suddenly intrigued. What is she like outside working hours? Is she this icy, and does she always wear pantsuits?

"Take care, Mr Kobe." She turns on her heel and walks off before I can say anything else. I chuckle to myself. She walks like a soldier marching into battle.

After work, I head to a restaurant to meet with Steph. I had almost forgotten about it when Becky reminded me. She's not a fan of Steph, ~~but~~ apparently, Steph had called a few times, and it was irritating Becky.

Steph arrives a little late in a tight-fitting pink dress that leaves nothing to the imagination. The colour complements her dark skin, and the dress emphasises her hourglass figure.

"How was your day?" I ask her. I still don't know what she does.

"It was fine. Mum and I went to the spa. I really needed it, you know." She puts her hand on her neck. "I had so much tension which needed to be released." She runs her hand down her neck, giving me dreamy eyes. I should be turned on, but I'm wondering why I'm even here.

Our food arrives, and we eat over a dreary conversation. She talks a lot, and it's mostly about herself. I have gathered that she doesn't work. She lives off her parents. I'm not going to ask what her parents do; I'm not interested.

She keeps leaning in a way that reveals her cleavage. She doesn't have to try too hard. Steph has ample cleavage, unlike Eve. Eve has small breasts which get buried underneath her blazer. I've caught glimpses of her curves, but she's always in pants. I wonder if she ever wears skirts or dresses. I'm sure she'd look good in something short. Going by her height, I'd bet she has lovely long legs.

Steph cuts into my thoughts when she calls my name. "Shall we get out of here?" She says. I know what she wants, but I don't want to give it to her.

"Stephanie, you're a gorgeous woman," I say.

"I know." She smiles and tucks a lock of hair behind her ear.

"If we had met at a different time, things would've worked out."

"What are you saying?" She spits out.

"The timing isn't right for us."

"You don't want to see me anymore?"

"I-"

She waves me off. "You're rejecting me? All of this." She runs her hand down her body. I clear my throat.

"To be honest, I wasn't happy with how you spoke to my assistant. It revealed what kind of a person you are."

She frowns. "This is about her?"

"It was the last straw. We aren't right for each other."

"You'll regret this." She gets up and walks off.

**

I get a sick feeling in my stomach as I arrive at the familiar doorstep in Chelsea. I've never been able to break with a woman cleanly. I sigh as I press the doorbell. A smartly dressed woman opens the door for me.

I follow her into the house and straight to the balcony. John welcomes me with a smile and a handshake.

"I'm glad you could make it. This is my wife, Sharon," he says. I look at the beautiful older woman standing at his side. She's dressed up and wearing expensive jewellery. A bit extra for a Saturday lunch at her house, but that's how my ma is too.

"Pleasure," I kiss her on the cheek.

"The pleasure is all mine," she beams.

"These are my children," he waves. I turn to see who he's waving over. Fuck me. "This is my son Edward and my daughter Stephanie."

Yes, it's the same Stephanie I broke up with a few days ago. This is not good. She looks at me right in the eye as she approaches. She's dressed up as always, and she looks good.

"Hello," she extends her hand. I shake it warily. "It's nice to meet you, Mr Kobe," she says.

"Likewise." I'm lost on why she's pretending not to know me, but I don't care. Sharon is watching with a mischievous smile on her face as if she knows something ~~know~~ no one else does.

"Henry, it's good to meet you," Edward gives me a weak handshake. John enters the house and comes back with two glasses of whiskey.

"Twenty-five-year-old Scottish single malt whiskey," he says, handing me a glass. "Cheers." He clinks my glass, and we both drink. It's strong, but it's good.

I almost drop my glass when my eyes land on Eve as she approaches. She's wearing a halter neck navy jumpsuit which embraces her small pear-shaped figure. I have a feeling her wardrobe contains only dark clothes.

"Hello, everyone," she says. Her pixie cut is styled with a side parting and sleeked down to the side. She's not wearing any make-up, but her skin ~~is~~ still glorious. I notice her long eyelashes.

"Eve, welcome!" John stands by her side. "This is my wife Sharon, you've met my son, and ~~that's~~ this is my daughter Steph."

"Nice to meet you all," she replies with her signature icy look. I gaze at her, and she notices. She holds my gaze. No smile, nothing. I wonder why she has such a tough exterior. I want to break down her walls and see what's inside. I want to melt ~~this~~ her iciness.

I want her, all of her.

← this doesn't make sense actually

Chapter 10

Eve

The way he's looking at me makes my stomach knot up. I want to look away, but I'm hypnotised by his hazel gaze. My breath is suddenly jammed up in my throat. This doesn't happen to me. What kind of shit is this?

"Nice to meet you, Eve," Sharon says. I'm grateful for her speaking and interrupting this awkward moment. I look at her. She's gorgeous and dressed elegantly. I see where Stephanie gets her looks from. She's tall and beautiful, just like her mother.

The lady that ushered me into the house comes to tell us that lunch is ready. We follow her to the dining room. We sit down at the marble top table. ~~with~~ a crystal chandelier hanging above.

John sits at the head of the table and Sharon at the foot. Stephanie rushes to sit next to Henry as if someone was fighting her for the seat. I find myself sitting next to Ed. Great. I hope he doesn't speak to me; he just rubs me up the wrong way. I didn't come here to socialise. When John invited me over, I knew I had to come. It was my chance to gather any information I could.

We're served with ridiculous portions of food. I assume they're appetizers, but I'm wrong. I make a mental note to buy food on my way home because Becky would have prepared salads or some crap like that. I swear she wants to turn me into a rabbit.

"Are you seeing anyone?" Sharon asks Henry.

"No," he looks uncomfortable with the question. I'm wondering if that's an honest answer or not. A man like him can't be single.

"That's a surprise. A young handsome, and successful man like yourself should settle down."

"You sound like my mother."

"You need to listen to us."

Fake laughs fill the room. I don't laugh or smile. This isn't my usual crowd, and I know I'm sticking out like a sore thumb in my cheap jumpsuit. On the other hand, Stephanie is wearing designer labels with fake lashes and nails. She's dolled up as if she's going somewhere.

Ed is also dressed up, but his outfit makes him look like a twat, or maybe it's because I get easily irritated by him. He gets his perfect dark skin tone from his mother. He's texting, probably someone's daughter. He has no manners. Sharon shoots him a scowl, and he puts his phone away.

John starts retelling his success story of how he rebuilt his company after he took over from his father. The company was close to going bankrupt, but he saved his company through his hard work and determination. He aims the conversation at Henry. Clearly, John wants to impress him. I'm not impressed; he built his company off the backs of too trusting people.

I sit there, watching him speak with so much joy and pride. His wife beams at every word he utters. Ed and Steph are entitled brats who don't seem to care for the story. And I am just here watching my father, yes, my father speaking of how he did everything he could to save his family's legacy and how he'd do anything for them,

As we eat, Sharon keeps stealing glances at me. I don't know what that is about. I also notice Stephanie grazing Henry's arm every chance she gets, whether she's passing the salt or picking up her cutlery. I fight the urge to narrow my gaze at her. I just don't know why women do things like that. Henry, on the other hand, seems to take no notice.

"You look familiar. Have we met before?" Sharon says to me.

"I doubt that," I reply.

"Where did you grow up?"

"North London." I lie.

"Do your parents live there?"

"They passed away when I was little." Technically true.

"Oh, I'm sorry. How did they die?"

Fucksake. Why is she asking so many questions? I need to shift the attention from myself.

"Car accident." I take a swig of the nasty overpriced wine they served. I'm not much of a drinker anyway.

"If you ever need anything, don't hesitate." John gives a reassuring smile, but I don't return his smile. I can't. My hand forms a fist under the table. I'd love to land it in someone's jaw, but that's too easy. I will strike where it hurts. Their beloved company.

I'm happy when the lunch comes to an end. I ask to go to the restroom, and one of the housekeepers escorts me. I wish she hadn't, but all I can do now is eyeball my surroundings, taking note of where everything is.

"Thank you for inviting me over," I say to John and Sharon. It's time for me to leave; I've already been here long enough.

"How are you getting home?" Henry asks me.

"Tube."

"I'll give you a lift."

I catch a glimpse of Stephanie in the background watching the exchange with a frown on her face.

"You don't have to."

"I insist." He shakes John's hand and walks out before I can argue.

"See you Monday," John says to me. Then retreats into his house and shuts the front door. I rush down the stairs.

"I'll be alright on the tube," I say to Henry, standing at the passenger's side with the door open. He gestures for me to get it. "Okay." I sigh and get in. He waits for me to be comfortable before closing the door.

The seats are maroon leather and very comfortable. I notice how clean the car is on the inside. This may seem like a strange thing to notice, but some people chuck a lot of stuff in their back seats.

"Where do you live?" Henry asks as he sticks the key into the ignition, causing an impressive roar.

"You can drop me off at the tube," I answer. His cologne fills up the car, and it smells glorious. He raises an eyebrow at me. Clearly, I'm not going to win this one. "Hammersmith."

"Okay."

I steal a glance as he looks in the other direction. His profile is impressive as his portrait. I take notice of his well-kempt beard. He is simply dressed in a polo shirt and chinos, but the attire looks good on him. He turns and meets my gaze. Crap!

"Like what you see?" he gives me a mischievous smile. I look away.

"Just wondering why you're giving me a lift." That was the first I could think of saying, and I know it sounds lame.

"It's just a lift."

"You might have plans."

"I don't."

Shocking. Expected him to be having dinner with somebody's daughter. Henry puts the radio on.

"Music?" he asks.

"It's your car."

The car is filled up with 90s R n B.

"What?" I can't help but laugh a little. He stops at the traffic lights and looks at me in shock.

"What's wrong with this song?"

"I didn't expect this type of music from you."

He raises an eyebrow. "What kind of music did you think I listened to?"

I shrug. "I don't know."

He starts singing, *"And next time you come my way, I know just what to say. Can we talk for a minute? Girl, I want to know your name."*

He's looking at me as he sings, and I can't take it. I look away. His voice sounds so beautiful. I know he's not singing to me or about me, but I feel a flutter in my stomach.

"It's nice to hear you laugh," he says. I look at him with my eyebrows raised.

"Huh?"

"You're always so serious."

"Am I?" I look straight ahead.

"Yes, Ms Gutu."

"You can just call me Eve, you know."

"Hmm, I like Ms Gutu, the ice queen."

"The who?" My eyebrows knit together as I glare at him. He's giving me nicknames now.

"We don't even talk anymore. We don't even know what we argue about. Don't even say I love no more."

He's back to his singing. Damn this traffic! It's allowing him time to sing, looking at me in the face. I look away because I will blush if I keep looking at him.

I'm happy but a little bit sad when we arrive at my place. His voice was growing on me.

"Thank you for the lift," I say. Henry hands me his phone. I look at it and then look at him.

"May I have your number? For when I need to reach you." The combination of his deep voice and his piercing gaze makes me want to melt into the seat. I clear my throat and gather myself.

"Your assistant has my number; she can always reach me if you need anything."

He narrows his gaze at me. I don't think that was the answer he was expecting. I don't know why he'd need to reach himself, anyway. Becky can do that. I blink a few times. Why is he affecting me so much?

"Thanks, okay, ciao." I climb out of the car and head into the block of flats.

Ciao? What the heck was that? When have I ever said ciao? I'm so embarrassed. I get in the lifts and lean against the wall with my hand on my heart. It's pounding so hard as if I just ran a marathon.

Christ, what has Henry done to me?

Chapter 11
Henry

After my morning run and a shower, I find myself driving to Hammersmith. I park outside the familiar building and pull out my phone. Thanks to Becky, I have *her* number. I've never been rejected so cleanly before, or ever! Eve flat out refused to give me her number. I can't wait until the next we meet, the next time I see her. It could be months; there's nothing scheduled yet between John and me. I can't wait that long. I want to see her today, now.

Morning, Ms Gutu. I send a message. I wonder if I should've called instead. What if she takes forever to reply? I check the time, it's 10 am. She should be awake by now.

Who's this? She responds quicker than I thought she would. There's no profile picture on her messenger; I can't even say I'm surprised.

Come outside and find out, ice queen.

I frown as soon as I send the message. She probably won't come out now. She must be thinking there's a crazy stalker or something.

The message is blue ticked, and she doesn't respond. Great! She thinks I'm psycho, and she'll block me now. I sigh and look out of the window. I've never had problems when it came to women. Now here I am, second-guessing my every move.

Just then, the entrance door swings open and out comes Eve. She's wearing leggings and a baggy sweater. She looks around until her gaze lands on my car. She scowls and then walks over. I press the button, and the window rolls down at the passenger's side, and I smile at her.

"Henry?" She looks confused.

"Morning," I say. She frowns.

"What's going on? Is there an emergency?"

"Nope."

"Erm, okay? So, what are you doing here?" She doesn't mince her words.

"Get in."

"Huh?"

I lean over and open the door. She sighs and then gets in and shuts the door. Her hair is a bit messy, which I strangely find adorable.

"Have you had breakfast?" I ask.

"No."

I expected her to say yes. She seems like such an organised person who wakes up very early to take a shower and get started on her day.

"Good." I start the car engine. I'm not going to risk asking her if she wants to eat because then she might just say no.

"Where are we going?" she whips her head in my direction.

"Breakfast," I flash a grin. She draws in a deep breath, she's frustrated, but I want to laugh. The car starts alarming, prompting her to put on her seatbelt. She does so, and I just step on the gas.

"I didn't think you would come out. What if I was a crazy person or something?"

"You are crazy," she mumbles, but I hear her. I gasp. "Besides, I thought it was you. You're the only person who calls me ice queen."

"Mhmm." And I want it to stay that way.

"Which I don't understand why you call me that." She turns to face me.

"You're always stern-looking and never smile, laugh, or even sneeze."

She narrows her gaze at me and looks away. I can tell she's holding back what she wants she really wants to say. "We've only met in a professional capacity. There was never a reason for me to laugh," she says.

"We're not meeting in a professional capacity today," I say, parking up outside Westfield. She raises an eyebrow.

"What are we doing here?"

"Having breakfast, I'm starving." I climb out of the car, but she still sits there confused. I walk around and open the door for her. She warily gets out.

"Where is good to eat?" I ask her as we head into the mall. She shrugs her shoulders.

"I don't come out for breakfast."

I'm not surprised. We stop at the first restaurant we see and go in. A waitress greets us and ushers us to an empty table. She gives us menus and sashays off. Eve doesn't pick up her menu; she glares at me instead.

"If we're not here in a professional capacity, then why are we here?" She asks. I meet her confused glare.

"I wanted to have breakfast with you."

It doesn't seem enough for her. "Where did you get my number?"

I grin. "What would you like to have?" I look at my menu.

"Becky," she mumbles. She picks up her menu. "A full English."

The waitress returns to take our orders. I watch Eve giving her order. She's polite and straight to the point with what she wants. I give my order too, and then the waitress heads off. She brings our coffee while we wait for food.

"What are your plans for the day?" I ask Eve.

"Well, I was in bed when you messaged." She doesn't sound happy about being disturbed. I raise an eyebrow.

"You sleep in?"

"It's Sunday; of course, I sleep in!"

"What else do you do on a Sunday?"

She shrugs her shoulders. "I was just planning on staying in bed and binge-watching something today."

"We can still do that." I tease. Her eyebrows shoot up.

"Who's we?"

Damn, she's not going to make it easy for me. A beautiful challenge. I laugh at her response.

"Putting it simply, I want to spend time with you and get to know you. Not because of business but personal reasons."

"Personal reasons." She eyes me with suspicion. Just then, the waitress brings our food. I watch Eve as she eats. Unlike Steph, she enjoys her food and doesn't order salads. She looks up and meets my gaze. She looks at me with an expressionless face for a moment. It's clear she doesn't know what to make of me yet.

"What's a typical Sunday for you then?" she asks.

"I go for a run in the morning, shower, eat, go to my parents for a Sunday roast."

"Oh." She says plainly.

"What?"

"Roast with the parents; I didn't expect that."

"Ma wouldn't have it any other way."

"Mama's boy." She teases with a straight face. I chuckle in response. She has dead-pan humour.

"Tell me about your family."

"There's nothing to tell." Her face has hardened. I want to know everything about her, but I don't push. Right now, she doesn't feel comfortable around me and has no reason to open up to me.

I pay for our breakfast when we're finished eating, and then we leave the restaurant. I open the car door for her. She warily gets in and buckles her seatbelt. I shut the door and climb in from the other side. I switch on the stereo and start singing twisted, looking at Eve. She has got me twisted for sure. I haven't known her for long, nor have I spent much with her, but she's got me twisted.

She attempts to hold my gaze with a stern look as I sing to her. I shorten the distance between us as I continue singing, fighting back the urge to introduce my lips to hers. They're not too thin and not too thick. I wonder if they're as soft as they look.

Eve leans forward and changes the song.

"let's make love tonight," I sing. She shakes her head and looks away. I can see a smile threatening her lips, but she fights it.

"Why is it only 90s love songs on your playlist?"

"I have 80s, 00s too."

She changes the song again, and just her luck, it's another love song. I intentionally chose that playlist.

"It's 7 o'clock in the dark" This time I'm dancing. A hearty laugh bubbles out of her beautiful mouth, instantly warming my insides. Her laugh is music to my ears. At that moment, I swear to keep her laughing like that. She's gorgeous when she laughs.

"Can we go?" She requests. I grant her request. The one time I hope for traffic, the world lets me down. The roads are clear, and we're back at hers in under ten minutes.

"Thank you for breakfast," she says as I park up.

"My pleasure, let's do it again soon," I reply. By soon, I mean tomorrow. Her eyebrows slowly rise. She probably thinks I'm up to something. I see the distrust in her face.

"Enjoy the rest of your day, Mr Kobe," her tone matches her icy face. She climbs out of the car and heads into her building.

The unfamiliar taste of rejection graces my lips, and I don't like it. Wooing her will be a lot harder than I thought, but I'm ready. I am a Kobe, and we don't rest until we get what we want.

And I want her.

Chapter 12
Eve

"Where did you go?" Becky asks as I scurry in.

"You gave Henry my number," I say.

"Yeah, he said he had something to discuss with you. I figured it's okay since you'll be doing business with him."

I sigh loudly. Business to discuss, alright. I head to my room and throw myself on the bed. I put my hand on my beating heart. Traitor. For whatever reason, the treacherous thing is beating fast again. It's never been like that, not for anyone. Now I spent a measly hour with him, and it's beating as if I've run a race.

I keep trying to figure out why Henry basically ambushed me and took me out for breakfast. I don't know what he meant by let's do it again soon. Today was the first and last time we did that.

"EVE AMARA CHARI!"

Fuck. I sit up fast. Why is gogo full-naming me? What have I done? My bedroom door swings open, and in walks an angry elderly woman. I get off the bed and stand out of arms reach from her. She's flustered, and I don't want to catch a whooping.

"Afternoon gogo," I say nervously. She's all dressed up, and her hair has been roller-curled. Wait a minute, it's Sunday. Is she here to drag me to church? It's been a while since I've been. She keeps reminding me to go, and I still haven't followed instructions.

"How could you?"

"What did I do?"

I duck as a one-inch heel flies towards me. Damn, she's quick.

"Gogo, at least tell me what I did wrong!"

I see Becky in the background, watching but not coming too close because she knows gogo will beat both of us if she must. Gogo sees Becky as her granddaughter, so she loves both of us but will also discipline both of us.

"Who are you working for?"

Fuck. How did she find out?

"Huh?" I feign ignorance. I will deny it with everything I have.

"Rebecca, come in here."

Oh no!

"Yes, gogo," Becky rushes over.

"Tell me again who she works for!" Gogo barks.

Becky wants to kill me. Why did she tell gogo? Why?

"Kasi implants."

"You told her?" Now I'm fuming.

"What?" Becky shrugs her shoulders.

"Give us privacy."

"Eve, what-

"Becky, go." I grit my teeth. She scurries away, confused.

"Quit that job immediately," Gogo orders.

"I can't."

"What is it, Eve? Did I not love you enough? Why would you go to *him?* Was I not enough?"

"You are my everything, gogo."

"Then what is it?"

I look down. I don't want to tell her; I can't. She'll stop me. I duck quickly as the other shoe comes flying. I feel the draft as it skins my face. I side-eye the fire escape across the room and wonder how long it would take me to jump over the bed and make it to the fire escape. I will not die in this room.

"Do you not know what he did?" She asks.

"Gogo, I know, but I'm not there to reconnect with him. I grew up without a father; I don't need one now."

"So, why would you go and work for your father?"

"He's not my father."

She sighs. "Oh, Eve." She approaches me, and I'm wary. I glance at the fire escape again. She holds my shoulders and searches my eyes. "Tell me what you're up to, now." A soft yet threatening command. She could always see through my lies, but right now, I need to deter her from enquiring further.

"I was just curious about what kind of a man he is. It's a temporary post anyway. I won't stay for long."

She sighs. "How much longer?"

"A month." That's all I need. She nods and walks around me, and collects her shoes. She didn't order me to pick them up, so I know she's not okay. She puts on her heels and heads for the door.

"Gogo?"

"Bye Eve," and without a backward glance, she exits my room. For the first time in a long time, I want to cry. She seems hurt. She thinks I'm searching for my father's love because she wasn't enough for me. It's not true; gogo is my everything. She raised me, loved and took care of me. She was my mother, father and grandmother.

I'm angry at Becky for telling gogo where I work. Like how did it even come up in conversation?

"John Kasi is your father?" Becky stands in the doorway.

For goodness' sake. She heard?

"No." My fists ball up at my side.

"That's why you were angry that I told gogo where you work."

"Why did you even tell her?"

"She called this morning when you were out, and she was asking about you and how your new job is."

I run my hand through my hair. I'm mad as hell right now. I can't have everything fall apart before I have even begun to get my revenge.

"Why did she call you Eve Amara Chari?" Becky questions. And now she knows my real name. Great!

"Nevermind," I attempt to dismiss her, but she's having none of it.

"No, Eve, what's going on?"

"None of your business, okay?"

She's quiet for a moment and then turns on her heel. She suddenly stops in her tracks and whips her head in my direction.

"Were you trying to score a contract between Henry and John to impress your father?"

"Becky, let it go." I grit my teeth. Her perfectly threaded eyebrows knit together.

"It seems like you kept a lot of things from me. Are we even friends, or was I just a necessary vessel for you to get to Henry?"

I say nothing.

"Wow, Eve," she shakes her head and storms out.

"Becky!" I call after her. Damnit. I've just pissed off the two people that give a damn about me, and I don't know how to fix it.

I can't afford to step away from John now. He must pay for ruining my life.

Chapter 13
Eve

Gogo isn't answering my calls, and Becky is ignoring me. I know it was selfish of me to start a friendship with Becky just because she worked for Henry. It initially started off that way, but overtime, she became that annoying sister I never had.

Becky and I met a few years ago after learning who my father was. Gogo finally decided to tell me about my father and why he was never in my life. With hate fuelling me, I devised a plan to get back at him for ruining my life. I read everything I could about him and found out that he had been trying to work with Henry Kobe.

I read up about Henry and saw a picture of him and Becky. So I stalked her and spotted an opportunity when she fell over in the road, and I helped her up. I took her to the bus stop, and we got on the same bus. We weren't going in the same direction, but I lied that I was just so we could talk and ended up swapping numbers. We have been friends since then.

"Oi!" A shrill voice brings me out of my thoughts.

"Stephanie," I say.

"My father raves on about how good you are at your job, but here you are daydreaming."

"Your father's not in at the moment."

She sits on my desk and crosses her legs, revealing her thick dark thighs. She has a nice body, but her dress leaves nothing to the imagination. I lean back in my seat and glare at her. I don't know what she wants, but I'm not in the best of moods. So, she better make it snappy and get out of my face.

"Where did Henry drop you off on Saturday?" She asks. It's about Henry? I knew she was into him. Even a blind man could see that.

"At my house."

She frowns. "Next time, just ask me, and I'll give you cab fare."

"As opposed to getting a lift from him?"

"Bingo!"

Oh, she's marking her territory. I don't bother responding to her nonsense, but she keeps glaring at me, expecting me to. I suppress the urge to roll my eyes at her.

"Keep an eye on him for me and let me know if any women are in his company."

I narrow my gaze at her. She's beautiful yet insecure. Firstly, she warns me off him, and now she wants me to keep an eye on him.

"I have better things to do."

"Argh," she rolls her eyes and opens her purse. She pulls out a wad of cash. "I'll pay you."

And I'll smack you! She's so arrogant and annoying.

"I don't need your money." I check the time, and thankfully, it's lunchtime. I spring up to my feet.

"Argh, you're a piece of work." She gets on her feet too. "All I'm saying is Henry, and I are together, and I just need a lookout. It would bode well for you to attend to my needs."

She sashays off into the lift. I'm left standing there with my nose flaring. I'm more annoyed at her saying she's with Henry than being offered money like a charity case. Are those the type of women he's into? I find myself wanting to get the truth from the horse's mouth.

Crap! I almost forgot. I pull out a small recording device and rush into John's office. I stick the little bug underneath his desk and quickly make my exit.

I get a message on my phone. *Lunch? Ms Gutu?* The message reads. I guess let's do it again soon meant today. I'm in a bad mood today, and maybe he is the distraction I need.

Okay, where shall we meet? I respond.

Hyde Park.

I call John and tell him that I'm going out for lunch and check if he needs anything from me. Fortunately, he doesn't. I hastily make my exit and arrive in Hyde Park fairly quickly.

I spot a tall, handsome dark man leaning against the streetlamp when I exit the station. His white crisp white shirt hugs his muscles nicely. I get closer and inhale his manly cologne. He looks up and meets my gaze. A smile immediately forms on his beautiful lips.

"My ice queen is right on time. Part of me thought you wouldn't come," his gruff voice makes my stomach flutter in response. I don't miss the fact that he called me HIS ice queen. Whatever that's about. He probably misspoke.

"Ice queen," I narrow my gaze at him. He smiles and starts walking. I start walking too. He offers his arm to me. Something tugs at my heart. No man has ever offered me their arm. As crazy as it sounds, I've never walked down the street with my arm linked into another man's arm. I reject his offer and look away.

We go into a high-end restaurant, the type I'd never go to eat at. Henry pulls out my chair for me. I don't need anyone to do that for me, but he's already done it. So, I just sit. There aren't many people in the restaurant, which makes sense when I see the food prices.

"What would you like to have?" he asks me.

"I have no idea," I admit. I put the menu down. "I'll have whatever you're having."

He nods and places the orders for us. He gazes at me for a moment. "What's the matter?"

"With who?"

"You, you're not yourself."

What does he know about *myself*? "I'm fine." I lie, but he doesn't believe me. How the hell can he tell? "I don't want to talk about it."

"It might make you feel better." I don't believe it will, but his hazel gaze lures me in, and I tell him that I had a tiff with a friend and my grandmother. He listens to me as I talk. I don't give him details of the fights, though.

"Are you in the wrong?" he asks.

"Eh..." my voice trails off. I am, but I hate admitting that. My eyeballs nearly fly out of their sockets when I suddenly feel his warm and soft hands taking mine into them.

"Your hands are always cold." He teases. I know! But why point that out! I don't know why, but it's never bothered me before, but I'm now embarrassed. I try to snatch them away, but he holds me tightly and rubs my hands in an attempt to warm them up.

"Mr Kobe, this isn't professional," That's all I can say.

"It's not a business meeting," he retorts.

"Still."

"There's no conflict; my contract will be between John and me."

He got me there. I can't think of a response; I'm too distracted by the softness of his big hands.

"If you're in the wrong, apologise. It's clearly eating you up," he says softly. I sigh.

"I'm not good at that."

"What? Saying you're sorry?" He looks amused. I'm grateful for the waitress interrupting with our food. I take the chance to snatch my hands away. They actually feel a bit warmer.

Lobster for lunch! This is something new to me. The portions are small, but the food tastes good.

"Talk to your friend and explain why things happened the way they did and admit you're wrong." Henry is back on it. I nod. I'll try his way.

Lunch finishes quicker than I thought. He walks with me to the station. "Where are you going?" I ask.

"Back to work," he replies.

"With the tube?" I exclaim.

A soft chuckle comes out of him. "Yes."

"Oh," I'm surprised. Rich people take the tube?

"I take the tube, you know." As if he read my mind. He walks me to my platform and waits with me until my tube comes.

I sigh with relief when I'm in the comfort of the crowded tube and out of his company. The treacherous thing in my chest is beating fast. Again. I look at my hands and remember his touch. I liked it, but I couldn't let myself enjoy it.

**

I'm home and trying to make dinner for Becky. The dinner has carbs and fats! She'll have to forget about her diet tonight. I don't even know why she is on it. She's about a size 12, toned, with beautiful almond skin and curly hair. She doesn't need to change anything. I hear the front door slam, and I rush into the living room.

"Becky, we need to talk," I say.

"There's nothing to talk about." She starts going to her bedroom, but I run after her, pick her up and slam her down on the sofa. "Eve, what the hell!" she cries out.

I sit on her legs and pin her arms down. I don't know how to be soft and warm. I want to apologise and explain like Henry told me to, but I have to pin her down for her to listen. I hate chasing after people, and I hate repeating myself.

"Yes, John is my father, but I'm not there to reconcile with him. Yes, I knew you worked for Henry when we met, and I wanted you to help me get a meeting with Henry, but I genuinely became your friend along the way. I made dinner; can we talk over food?"

Humour graces her face. "You cooked?"

I get off her. "I can cook, you know. Gogo taught me, but I just hate doing it."

We head to the kitchen, and Becky sits down and lets me dish up for her. I dish for myself, and then I sit down too.

"My mother worked for John, and that's how they met. John's father wanted his son to marry into a wealthy family at that time. So, John was already engaged to marry Sharon. He fell in love with my mother and refused to marry Sharon. Sharon's family threatened to pull their investments from John's family businesses if he didn't marry Sharon. John and Sharon stitched up my mother for embezzling money and falsified documents. She was sentenced to three years in jail. They didn't know that she was pregnant with me at the time." I sigh and take a swig of my drink. This brisket I grilled is banging, if I should say so myself. Becky is staring at me, waiting for me to continue.

"I was born in prison, but my mother didn't make it. She suffered an amniotic fluid embolism and died. So Gogo raised me," I say. Tears flow down Becky's cheeks.

"I'm sorry," She says. I raise an eyebrow.

"Why are you crying?"

"It's so sad how your life began; I'm so sorry."

I shrug. "John and Sharon will pay," I say plainly. She wipes her tears and stares at me with a stone-cold face. I've never seen her like that.

"Let's make them pay." Her voice has dropped a few decibels, giving me chills.

I'm in bed feeling lighter than a feather. I'm glad I came clean to Becky. She surprised me with her reaction. She's willing to help with whatever I need. I don't want to drag her into my mess just in case everything goes south. Her loyalty is enough.

I find myself retrieving my phone from the nightstand and sending a message to Henry.

I explained and apologised. I instantly regret it as soon as I send the message. Why am I even reporting back to him?

And how did it go? He replies faster than I expected.

She's forgiven me.

How do you feel?

Better.

Good. Well done for admitting that you were in the wrong.

Well done? I frown as I send the message. I'm not a child. I don't need to be told, well done, you did well.

Yes, my ice queen. Well done, you did well. You did something you felt uncomfortable doing. I'm proud of you.

Proud of me? The only other person who's said that to me before is Gogo. It feels weird receiving those words from Henry. I decide not to respond. I shouldn't have bothered to message him, and he needs to stop calling *his* ice queen. I'm neither, not an ice queen and certainly not HIS.

Chapter 14
Henry

"You can't go in!" Brenda, my father's secretary screams. I raise an eyebrow. Why is she being so hysterical?

"What's the matter?" I ask.

"He's, erm, busy."

"Erm, is he?" I imitate her. Why is she stuttering?

I march into my father's office and walk in on him standing by the window speaking to someone. They both have their back towards the door. They turn when I walk in, and my father looks as if he was caught doing something he shouldn't. I look at the man standing next to him.

"What's going on?" I ask. I eye up the unfamiliar bloke from head to toe. He's tall, dark and slim. He has a small neat afro and a goatee. The resemblance between my father and him is striking.

"Henry, what are you doing here?" he looks flustered.

"What's going on, dad?"

He sighs and hangs his head. "You were always going to find out," he mutters.

"Find out what?"

The bloke steps towards me and stretches his hand out. "Matthew." He says. I shake his hand warily.

"Henry."

"We're brothers."

"What the fuck?"

I look at my father for an explanation, but he rubs his eyebrows. "Dad?" I say. I need him to start talking.

"Son, Matthew is your older brother," he says at last.

"What?" I'm so confused. I am the oldest child. Where did Matthew come from?

"I just found out about him. I was going to tell you."

"Who's his mother? Why are you only just founding out?"

"Lynett. She was our maid for a while."

"Our? Yours and ma's? So, you were already married to ma when you slept with his mother?"

My father nods. I can't stand here any longer. I'm angry and disgusted. I will kick someone's face in if I stay here any longer.

"Son, wait!" My dad calls after me, but I keep storming off. "Your mother doesn't know."

I look at him with disappointment and anger smeared on my face. I looked up to this man. How could he do this to my mother?

I punch and punch the punching bag, but my anger isn't alleviated. Boxing is usually the best thing to dissipate my anger, but it's not working today. So, I leave the house and go on a drive. A long speedy drive should do it. Nope! I find myself parked outside Eve's building.

I want to bash my head against the steering wheel. Why did I come here? I haven't spoken to her for a week now. The last time we spoke, she had messaged me, which caught me off guard. Then she just didn't reply anymore. It's like every time I get close, she backs up. She has a wall up and won't let me in. She won't let me get to know her.

Without thinking, I just call her number. With each ring, a piece of my heart shatters. Just when I'm about to give up, she answers.

"Hello?" That soft alto voice, I had missed it.

"Eve," I say plainly. No ice queen, no Ms Gutu. I'm all out of goofiness.

"What's going on? It's 10pm. Why are you ringing me so late?"

I'm quiet for a moment. I know it's late, but here I am outside her building. I don't even know which flat she lives in. I should've gone for a drink instead. Coming here was a bad idea. I'm about to taste rejection once again at her hands.

"Henry?" Her soft voice is now laced with concern.

"You should say my name more often." I sigh.

"What's going on?"

I'm silent again. "I shouldn't have called."

"But you did; why?"

"I'm outside."

"Outside where? My flat?"

She probably thinks I'm a stalker. "Mmhmm"

There's silence between us for a moment.

"I'm coming." The line goes dead. I don't believe what I just heard until I see her in tiny shorts and a hoodie running towards the car. She climbs in and sits next to me.

"Oh, shit. You came out." I give her a weak smile. Her perfectly shaped eyebrows knit together in concern. It's not often she shows emotions, and when she does, it's fleeting.

"What's wrong?" she asks. I shrug.

"Just fancied seeing your face."

She narrows her gaze at me. "Henry, what's going on with you? Stop making me repeat myself so much. This can't possibly have anything to do with work."

"And this is why you're an ice queen."

"Stop calling me that." She runs her hand through her messy hair. She was probably in bed when I called.

"I'm having a hard day." And she's not making it any easier right now. I want to be in her arms; instead, she's dishing out iciness. She rests her back against the door.

"I'm listening."

I hesitate. Then I tell her everything that happened with my father. She barely reacts, but there's a hint of shock on her face. She reaches out for my hand and changes her mind. She settles on tapping my shoulder. I burst into laughter.

"You're so awkward, oh my God." I can't stop laughing.

"What?" She's confused.

"So, you don't like apologising, you don't like repeating yourself, and you're awful at comforting people."

She looks at me as if I said something so offensive. "But you came to me. This is what you get."

"Damn." True to her nickname.

"I'm sorry you had to find out about your father. And now he's making you keep this secret from your mother."

"Mhmm."

"Men ain't shit."

My eyebrows furrow. I didn't expect her to say that. "Not all of us."

"Pshh. Why did you come to me? Why not Stephanie?"

"Who?"

"Stephanie Kasi."

"Why would I go to her?"

"She told me that you two were together."

I frown. "Nope, we're not." They talk?

"Does she know that?"

I chuckle and rub my eyebrows. "We went on a few dates, and that was that."

"Oh." I can't tell how she feels about that. I'm out so out of my depths with this woman. I don't know if she's feeling me or not. "Did you know she was John's daughter?"

"No. I only found out at that lunch."

"And that's after you had broken off things with her?" I nod. "That's awkward."

"She randomly brought me up in a conversation?" I want to know if they're close. I can't be entangled with friends.

"She wanted to pay me to keep an eye on any woman you're spending time with." Eve rolls her eyes. Okay, so she doesn't like Steph.

She switches on the radio. I watch her flipping through my playlists, avoiding any love songs. She settles on hip hop. "Maybe the radio will be better company for you than me right now."

I smile, "You're better." I take her hand, expecting her to snatch it away. "Your hands are cold."

"It's cold outside!" she snaps. I suppress a laugh as I bring her hand to my mouth and kiss it. Her eyebrows shoot up. I rub caress her cold hand. My ice queen.

Chapter 15
Eve

Henry is caressing my hand, looking at me as if he can see inside my soul. There's nothing but darkness in here, I want to tell him. Why does he insist on being like this?

"Am I your new toy?" Shit! I said that out loud. I want to kick myself.

"My toy? Why would you be?" He asks. Now I have to go with it. I can't let him see me sweat.

"Are you interested in me?"

"Yes."

Damn. Just like that? "Why?"

"Why not?"

"I'm icy, as you say. There's no warmth to me, and I know I didn't lead you on."

"You're beautiful, smart, feisty and very icy. I believe there's some warmth in you; I just have to find it."

"So I'm a challenge you need to complete?"

He shakes his head. "Can't a man just be interested in you? Why are you so doubtful and distrusting?"

I shrug because I have no answer for him. I don't trust anyone. He kisses my hand again. I want to tell him I've got work tomorrow and need to sleep, but the words don't come out. Instead, we sit in silence, holding hands and listening to music. And somehow, a bloody love song comes on, but he's not singing this time. I guess he's really having a bad day, and I haven't made it any better. I feel guilty, but I don't know how to be anything other than how I am.

His thumb caresses the back of my hand. Am I allowed to enjoy this? I'm not a friendly and lovable person. My heart is filled with hate. The promise of revenge propels my life. How can I make space for this beautiful man with warm hands?

I blink a few times until my mind registers where I am. I look at the man next to me, sleeping peacefully. I can't believe we fell asleep in his car. We're still holding hands. I check the time, and it's 4am. How did we sleep that long?

"Henry?" I say his name softly, but he doesn't wake up. I touch his arm; I try to ignore how big and toned his bicep feels against my hand. I shake him gently. A smile appears on his face when his gaze meets mine.

"Hey," he says.

"You have to go home; it's 4am."

"What?" he sits up, and I take the opportunity to take my hand back.

"Yeah, I know. I'll talk to you later." I get out of the car and run into my building.

**

I surprise myself later by messaging Henry asking how he is. I feel bad for not really being there for him last night. I don't know what the right things to say in that situation. We're not friends or lovers, and we're barely colleagues.

"Are you sure you don't want to come out with us?" Becky asks me, leaning in the doorway.

"No. Have fun." I barely look up. I just wave at her, and she leaves. She always invites me out when she's hanging out with her friends, but It's not my scene. My phone buzzes, and I pick it up quickly. There's a message.

Not great. Henry's response. Just two words, that's all he sent me. He's usually chatty. Now I don't know what to say or do. I bite my bottom lip as I think of what to say.

How can I help? I reply. I need him to tell me what I can do for him because I have no ideas.

Let me see you.

His response catches me off guard. I don't know what I expected him to say, but it wasn't that. How's seeing me going to help him.

I'm on my way. He messages. I haven't even agreed. He's persistent.

Okay.

Why is my heart beating faster? And why have I just agreed for him to come over?

He messages me half an hour later, telling me he's in the parking lot. I message him my door number. I regret it as soon I send the message. Now that he knows my house number, he can't unknow it now.

The doorbell rings, and I go to answer it. I see him standing before me in his grey slacks and a grey t-shirt. He gives me a faint smile. He's not his usual self, and I'm concerned.

"Come in," I say. This man has me acting out of character. "And take your shoes off."

"Okay." He does as I say. I gesture for him to sit down at the sofas, and he does. Now I don't know what to do. I'm good at running and fighting, I'm good with numbers and speak four languages. But I'm socially awkward. I dislike small talk; I don't like being in crowds, and I'm awful with people's emotions. I don't know how to comfort people.

I sit down next to him. I can't ask how he is because he's clearly not okay. I brought this awkwardness on myself.

"You're going through a lot," I say.

"Mhmm." He groans his response.

"I don't know how to help."

He looks at me and smiles. "You let me come over."

I shrug. Food! That makes some people feel better. "Would you like something to eat?"

"Yes."

"Okay. I'll see what we've got." I get up and go to the kitchen. I frown into the fridge. Did I just set myself up to cook? I shut the fridge and open the cupboards. Noodles! The answer to everything. Throw some bacon and an egg, and boom! You've got a tasty filling meal.

"I didn't take you for the cooking type." His deep voice yanks me out of my thoughts.

"I'm not; I hate it."

He laughs at me, and for an unknown reason, it warms my heart. "Then I'm honoured. What are you making?"

"Noodles." I put them in the pot, add some water and put the pot on the stove. I put some bacon on the grill and get an egg out of the fridge. He's watching me in fascination as I cook for him. I, EVE AMARA CHARI am cooking for a man. Who have I become?

"How was your day?" he asks me.

"Fine. Yours?" I dish out the food and hand him his bowl.

"Thank you. It was fine too." I don't believe his day was fine. He sees that I don't believe him. "I couldn't focus much on work. I couldn't stop thinking about seeing my father and Matthew. I don't know how I'll face ma."

"Has he called you?"

"Yeah, but I didn't pick up."

"Do your siblings know?"

He shakes his head. "This is an interesting combination. Tastes good."

I pour him a glass of water because Becky got rid of the juices and alcohol. She says it's better to eat fresh fruit than to drink juice. So, we're subjected to water. At least, tea and coffee are still allowed.

When he's finished eating, I put the bowl in the sink. I lean against the sink and look at him. "I'm probably not good company right now. I don't know what to do for people in such situations." I admit. Honesty. That's all I can offer. He'll have to forgive me for being a lame person. He shakes his head.

"Your company is what I need right now."

I laugh a little. "Really?" I don't believe that. He smiles, and the treacherous thing in my chest reacts.

"You have a beautiful laugh. You should laugh more."

"There's not much to laugh about."

"Why isn't there?"

I shrug. Today was meant to be about him, not me. I don't want him asking about me because I'm not going to tell him. I don't answer him. I just gaze at him, and he holds my gaze. He closes the distance between us and stops just a few inches from my face. The top of my head reaches his chin, so I tilt my head back a bit to maintain eye contact. I'm startled by his hand caressing my cheek. No man has ever been so gentle with me. I know it's a small gesture, but it's unfamiliar to me.

"You're so beautiful," he says. I know I'm not bad looking, but the way he says it. My stomach flutters, and I'm frozen. What do I do now? I can't let him in. I want to walk away, but it's as if he read my mind. He puts his hands on the sink, trapping me. He smells good.

"What are you afraid of?" he asks me.

"Who says I'm afraid of anything?"

"You keep me at bay. You have walls around you and won't reveal much about yourself. You seem to always be guarding your emotions, your thoughts. Let me in, Eve. Let me get to know you." His tone is soft, gentle, tempting.

"This is who I am, icy as you always say."

"Let me melt that ice." He's so cheesy. "Can I kiss you?" he moves closer, and our chests collide. I want to run, say something, do something, but I just stand here looking at him. His face is now inches from mine, and my eyes close. I feel the heat radiating from his face.

I feel his soft, warm lips gently press onto mine. I don't stop him. He presses another small kiss against my lips.

"Mr Kobe?" a familiar voice interrupts. Damnit! We both look at the door, and Becky is standing there with her mouth open.

"Becky?" Henry is just as shocked.

I thought she was going to be home later.

Chapter 16
Henry

"Becky, what are you doing here?" I ask.

"I live here." She replies. I look at Eve. She scratches the back of her neck awkwardly.

"Erm, we are housemates," she says.

"You live together?"

Eve nods. "For years."

"Mhmm." What are the odds?

"I should give you both some privacy." Becky is confused, and so am I. This is weird.

"I'll walk you out."

Eve walks me to the door. I was hoping she would walk me to my car, but I guess this is something.

"Have a good night," she says. I take her hand for a moment and caress the back with my thumb.

"You too." I smile before I leave. Coming here lifted my spirits. Though she doesn't say those cliché lines, she manages to bring me out of a foul mood. She took my mind off my father. Unfortunately, that's a situation I can't escape. I have to deal with it.

**

"So, you and Eve," I say to Becky over sandwiches. I bought her lunch so I could ask her about Eve. She's only just returned to work after having a few days off. I eagerly waited for her return so we could talk about Eve.

"We met a few years ago," she replies.

"Why didn't you tell me that you were friends?"

"I didn't think I needed to. I never thought there was something between the two of you."

I don't know if there's anything between us. We kind of kissed but were interrupted by Becky. I sent her messages during the week, and she replied here and there. I've never been this lost when it came to a woman. I don't know where I stand with her.

I open my mouth to speak when the door opens, and in walks Matthew. Becky springs up to her feet.

"Sir, you can't just walk in," she says.

"I'm sorry to interrupt." He says.

"Becky, please excuse us." I nod at her. She heads out of the room. Matthew makes himself comfortable in her seat.

"I thought we should talk." There's an air of arrogance around him.

"Why?"

"We are brothers, after all." I frown. "I'll cut to the chase. We share the same father, so I am also entitled to inherit this company."

"What?" I raise my eyebrows. He picks up a sandwich and takes a massive chunk out of it.

"As the eldest son, I should take over from him when he steps down."

"What?" I chuckle. He must be joking.

"Did I say something funny?"

"Yes, you did. I thought you said you should be the successor."

"I didn't stutter."

Oh, he is an arrogant opportunist, and I have no patience for his nonsense. "I worked alongside my father and helped him build this company to where it is today. There's no way you're going to be his successor."

He shrugs with a smug look on his face. "I just came to give you a friendly heads up." He gets up and looks around the office. "This office suits you better. I'll be at the headquarters in dad's office." He winks at me and leaves.

It hasn't even been two weeks since I found out about this twat, and now, he's trying to stake his claim in the company. One that I helped build. I won't let him take over, come hell or high water.

I call my dad, whose calls I had been avoiding, but now I have to speak to him.

"Hello?" he picks up.

"Your bastard was here," I say.

"I'm with your mother."

"I guess you haven't told her then."

He sighs. "I will."

"Please do it soon; otherwise, I will do it myself."

"Excuse me?"

"Oh, and by the way, if you think Matthew will be the next chairman, then you have another thing coming."

"Henry, what would make you think that?"

"That's what he thinks."

"Let's talk tomorrow."

I hang up. It's convenient for him if we talk tomorrow, a day before our weekly Sunday roast. I don't even know if I want to go home. I can't enjoy a roast prepared by my mother while keeping a secret that could rip our family to shreds.

I find myself outside of Eve's door later. Becky opens for me. "Hello," she says and opens the door wider for me.

"Hi Becky." I walk in. Eve walks out of the kitchen with a tub of ice cream in her hand.

"Henry?" She gasps.

"All of that?" Becky asks her.

"I think I've earned this."

"Eve!"

"Becky!"

I'm confused. Becky sighs.

"Fine. I'll be in my room." She walks off. I look at Eve in confusion.

"She has us eating like rabbits, and I'm struggling," Eve replies. I burst into laughter. Women and diets. She nods her head in the opposite direction for me to follow. I go with her to her bedroom.

"It's warmer in here," she says. Her room is clean and tidy. Everything has its place. I'm not surprised by her navy duvet and grey pillows. Eve is never in bright colours.

"I'm sorry to turn up announced. I can't seem to stay away from you."

She raises an eyebrow. "I should be used to your nighttime visits by now," she says, ignoring that I just said I cant stay away from her.

"You won't feed me today?" I eye the ice cream.

"I'll get you a spoon."

I shake my head and take the tub and spoon from her. She looks at me in disbelief as I eat with her spoon.

"Have you spoken to your father?" She asks.

"Kind of."

I tell her what happened with Matthew earlier. She shakes her head.

"You can't let him do that."

"I won't."

"I hate people that want things handed to them. It's not right. Have you told your siblings?"

"I can't bring myself to do that. My sisters will be heartbroken, and my brother, he's the crazy one. There's no telling how he'll react."

Eve is silent for a moment. "What's it like? Having siblings."

"I'm the eldest. So, I make sure they're okay, but they're annoying."

She smiles, but she looks sad. I want to know more about her family, about her. She's stingy with information.

"You finished my ice cream!" She cries out. That's the most emotion I've heard in her voice, and It's over food.

"Oh," I laugh in response.

"You'll buy me another." Her eyebrows are knitted together. She's passionate about her food. It's refreshing. I've been around women that are embarrassed to eat in my presence. They think eating salads is cute.

"Yes, ma'am."

Eve takes the empty tub, chucks it in the bin, and returns next to me. She leans against the headboard and laces her fingers together. She's in shorts and a hoodie again today. As I had expected, she has beautiful long legs. Her chestnut brown skin looks soft and glowy. I want to caress her thighs.

"Henry," she spits out. I look up and meet her gaze. "Stop staring at my thighs."

"Why are you single?"

"I never said I was." I cock my head to the side. She frowns slightly. "Why are you single?"

She deflects again. Getting her to open up is like getting blood out of a stone. "None of the women I met were right for me."

"And Stephanie?"

"I'm not with her, and I'm not interested. Does it bother you that I've been on dates with her?"

"It's not my business." He looks away. I think I just caught a glimpse of jealousy. Maybe there is hope for me. I scoot closer to her and put my head on her shoulder. She raises an eyebrow at me.

"Is Eve short for Evelyn then?" I ask. Seems like a stupid question, but I have to ask these random questions if I want to know her. She's not going to volunteer anything.

"No."

I take her hand. Even in the house, her hands are cold. I put her hand under my t-shirt.

"What are you doing?" Her eyebrows shoot up.

"Warming up your hands."

"Why are you always commenting on my hands?"

"Your tiny hands are always cold." She smiles and rolls her eyes at me. "Tell me, how did you grow up?"

She's silent for a moment. Pondering, no doubt. "There's not much to tell. My grandmother raised me."

"What was that like?"

"She's strict. The amount of times I got hit," she smiles. "It was just the two of us. She taught me so many things. She was my mother and father."

"Have you smoothed things over with her yet?"

She shakes her head. "I guess I'll need to ambush her in church, but I'll have to meet her boyfriend."

"She has a boyfriend?" I don't hide my shock.

"It's weird to me too. I don't know how to feel about it."

I laugh at her facial expression. I lay my head on her thighs, and she immediately pushes me off. Welp!

I'm not deterred, though. I knew she was going to be hard work. She looks at the time, and I know where this is going, but I'm not getting kicked out. I won't leave.

"I want to hold you," I say boldly. She sighs and gives me her hand. I smile and shake my head. "You not your hand."

She stares at me for a moment and then surprises me by moving closer. I pull her in and hold her tightly. I kiss her forehead. Her skin is soft, and she smells nice. I kiss her nose and then her cheek.

I run my hands down her back, she doesn't pull away. I kiss her softly. I'm gentle with her. She's like a possum; she rears her head and scurries back into her comfort zone. I don't know who hurt her or abandoned her, but they made it hard for her trust and love.

I kiss her lips, and she parts hers and kisses me back. It's slow, but I'm not in a rush. Our tongues meet, and I feel a jolt in my groin. I want her with every fibre of my being. She places her hand on my chest pulls back. I search her eyes and see her uncertainty.

"I want to be here with you," I say.

"I'm not having sex with you."

She knows how to pour ice-cold water on a man with her words.

Chapter 17
Eve

I'm looking into his hazel eyes, wondering what he's thinking. What does he mean he wants to be here with me? That could mean sex, right? He shakes his head.

"Not sex, not until you trust me and want me the way I want you," he says. His husky voice always has a way of making me feel some type of way. He smells good, and his body feels good against me. I'm feeling things I've not felt in a long time.

"Then what?" I ask.

"I want to lie here with you in my arms and wake up to your beautiful face."

He keeps calling me beautiful. Every time he says it, I'm tempted to believe him. The last man to call me beautiful said he was just being polite. I was too manly to be beautiful.

Henry kisses my hand and then unzips my hoodie. I want to protest, but nothing leaves my mouth. He takes my hoodie off and chucks it on the floor. I'm left exposed in my five-year-old sports bra. Lord, kill me now. It's lost all its elasticity, so I wear it at home. Henry lowers his gaze. I want to hide.

"I want to make love to you, but only when you're ready." He pulls me closer and kisses my forehead. I rest my head on his muscular chest and ponder his words. He wants to make love to me. Is it crazy that I want him to? But I'm wearing the world's most unattractive bra, I haven't shaved in months, and I haven't had sex in years.

I'm warm and comfortable. I open my eyes to check the time and find myself in Henry's arms. I can't believe I fell asleep in his arms and in my bed. I'm not sure they're many men that would sleep there with a woman and not try anything. I rest on my elbow and look at him. He looks peaceful in his sleep. Once again, I feel bad for not being the company he needed or deserved.

He opens his eyes, and our gazes meet. He instantly smiles. "Morning, beautiful," he says. His voice is throaty and deep.

"Hi," I reply. Instead of staring at him, I should've gone to change this bra. Now he's awake, and it's too late. He pulls me back into his arms, and I don't resist. He plants a small kiss on my forehead.

"How did you sleep?" he caresses my back.

"Fine, you?"

"Really well."

I frown. "Really well?" I question.

"Yeah." He moves me, and now I'm lying on my back. My head rests on his massive biceps. I knit my eyebrows and look at him, wondering what he's up to this time. He caresses my face and looks into my eyes before kissing me. I want to protest; I haven't brushed my teeth, but I welcome his lips instead. I kiss him back. He smiles as he searches my eyes.

He caresses my neck then runs his hand down to my thighs. He strokes my thighs. Meanwhile, my hands are flat at my sides.

"Do you want me to stop?" he asks for my consent. Words fail me. I just shake my head. I don't want him to stop. I just don't know how to welcome him. He cradles his head in my neck and kisses a spot that makes me feel powerless. A spot I never knew existed. His other hand finds my left breast and caresses it as he kisses me. A small moan escapes my lips.

He looks into my eyes as he caresses my breasts. I didn't even know how sensitive my nipples were. I look away as I moan again. I can't maintain eye contact while becoming moist like this. I'm suddenly feeling shy, an unfamiliar feeling to me. He puts his index finger on my chin and turns my head to him.

I look at him, but I'm blushing. He smiles and then kisses me. This kiss is different. It's faster, more passionate as if he's hungry for me. I'm left wanting more when he pulls away. He plants a kiss on my forehead. He pulls me into his chest and holds me. I'm all turned on now, but he's stopping; why? I look up to him, and he immediately smiles when he meets my gaze.

"Ms Gutu, I must stop now before I'm too aroused. I told you, I won't take you until you want me to." He says. But I want him to.

"Do I even turn you on?" I'm surprised as the words leave my mouth. I was meant to think that, not spit it out.

"So much more than you know. I have to control myself around you." As if he sees the doubt on my face, he takes my hand and puts in on his semi-hard manhood. My eyes fly wide open. I didn't expect him to do that, and I didn't expect him to be this well endeavored; he's not even fully aroused. I gasp. He laughs softly and brings my hand back to his chest.

"My mother's turning sixty in a few weeks. Can you be my date for the night?" he asks. I rest upon my elbow. I was still trying to process what my hand had just felt, and now he's talking about his mother. Great.

"Erm," I want to say no. Going to that party means meeting his family, and I'm not ready for that. I don't even know what we are to each other.

"Morning, gogo," I hear Becky's voice.

"Oh no!" I cry out and jump out of bed. "That's my grandmother; you have to go."

"What?" he climbs out of bed.

"She can't see you in my bed. She disagrees with sex before marriage. She'll whoop both our asses, trust me."

Henry starts laughing. I glare at him; there's no time for that. I just need him to go before gogo walks in here.

"Alright." He gets his shoes and keys. I push him towards the fire escape and open the door.

"You have to leave through here."

"What?" his eyes widen. I shrug my shoulders. He can't go through the living room. He'll bump into her. He nods and kisses me before he goes. I feel bad; it's starting to rain.

"What are you doing?" I hear gogo's voice as the door opens. I shut the door by the fire escape and turn to face her.

"Gogo, I was getting fresh air," I say. She doesn't seem to believe me, but she doesn't press further.

"What kind of a bra are you wearing?"

"What's wrong with it?"

"Child, you can afford to wear better undergarments. That thing is so old; please throw it out."

I suddenly feel self-conscious. What must've Henry thought when he saw it. I put on my hoody and sit down on the bed next to gogo.

"Are you still working for John?" She asks. I nod.

"But I've put in my notice." No, I haven't.

"Does he know who you are?"

"No. He thinks I'm Eve Gutu."

Gogo sighs. "I remember when your mother first brought him home. He was nervous; he seemed to really love her. Which is why I can't believe he did what he did to her."

"Men."

"Don't go thinking all men are evil. There are some good ones out there. When you find one, please hold onto him. Don't push him away."

I'm wondering if Henry is one of the good ones. He's patient and gentle with me. He could've had his way with me yesterday, but he didn't. How long will he be patient?

"Who is he?" Gogo asks.

"Huh?"

"Someone is occupying your thoughts." She knows me too well. I look down.

"Henry."

"What's the problem?"

"I don't know how to be with him."

"I don't know why you're so awkward. You certainly didn't inherit that from Amara."

Why does gogo have to be so savage? "I don't know how I feel about him yet."

She narrows her gaze at me. "You do."

I shake my head. "No," I argue.

She sighs. "If you didn't have feelings for him, you'd know. You never entertain anything you're not interested in. You're that impatient." She takes my hand. "What is he like?"

I shrug. "He's very patient with me."

"That's an important trait. How does he make you feel?"

Horny. "He's cheesy sometimes." I laugh. "He's always singing love songs, and it's annoying."

"You don't see that annoyed by it."

I frown.

"Anyway, we only just met. I'm still getting to know him." I deflect and look at the fire escape. I hope he descended okay. I wish he was still here in my bed and me in his arms.

I miss him.

Chapter 18
Henry

I'm a bit soaked when I reach my car. I can't believe Eve made me descend from a rusty first escape in the rain. She owes me!

I'm salty about her grandmother's untimely arrival. I wanted to spend the day with my ice queen. I hope they patch things up. She's all Eve's got. I want to be in the picture too. I want to be someone Eve can depend on, someone who'll be there for her and who'll move mountains to give her anything her heart desires.

**

I'm annoyed as I arrive at my parents' home for the Sunday roast. I was meant to meet with my father yesterday, but he was busy all day, a sudden meeting, he said. I find him in the drawing-room.

"Son," he looks up from his whiskey. My long strides eat up the distance between us quickly.

"I hate to have to do this now," I grit my teeth.

"Then, let's not."

"No, we're going to speak now. Matthew came to see me yesterday, and he said he wants a share of the company and that as the eldest, he should be the chairman."

My father sighs. He seems greyer than the last time I saw him. He takes a sip of his whiskey. "You'll still be the chairman."

Obviously. "But he'll still get shares in the company?"

"He's my son too."

"Unbelievable!"

"It wasn't my intention for things to be like this."

"Then what were your intentions when you landed between another woman's thighs while married to my mother?"

"I'm still your father; you'll address me with respect."

I don't even know if I still respect him. He finishes off his whiskey.

"It was one night only. I was drunk and Lynett, the maid, happened to be there."

I shake my head. Before I can speak, we're interrupted by Grace. "Lunch!" She calls out. I give my father a look to say we're not done. We follow Grace to the dining room and sit at the table. I don't even have an appetite. I don't want to be here.

"Henry, you have a guess," Karina; the head housekeeper, says. I turn and see Steph standing beside her. What the fuck!

"Young lady," My mother looks at Steph in confusion.

"Hello, I'm Steph, Henry's girlfriend," she says. Everyone looks at me wide-eyed. Fucksake! I don't want to embarrass her, but I can't let my family think we're together. Especially If I plan on introducing Eve to them in a few weeks.

"Well, have a seat." Ma gestures for Steph to sit down. "Karina, please set her a place."

"Steph and I are acquaintances." I clear my throat.

"Is that what they call it these days?" Faith jokes. I shoot her a glare. My father is quiet. Guilt probably. I hope it eats him up.

"How did the two of you meet?" Ma takes a swig of her drink.

"At the gym." Steph beams as she speaks. It feels like a lifetime ago. I was by the free weights, lifting when she approached and started talking to me. She gave me her number, and I called her days later.

I don't say much as we eat. Ma is watching Steph intently. Her gaze goes back and forth between Steph and me. I'm not even paying attention anymore. I just want this lunch to finish, so I can leave.

I go to the kitchen to have some water before I leave. Karina is sitting at the island counter preparing her shopping list for the week.

"You're not your usual self," she says to me.

"I'm fine." I take a gulp of water. She raises her eyebrow and watches me. I know she can see through me, but I can't tell her what set me off initially.

"Who's the young lady?" she nods in the direction of the dining room, and I gather she's referring to Steph.

"My girlfriend, you didn't hear?" My tone is drenched in sarcasm and irritation.

"She's gorgeous but doesn't suit you."

I laugh. Karina knows me too well, maybe more than my mother sometimes. Growing up, she knew about all my girlfriends, but ma didn't. She'd even reprimand me when I wronged my girlfriends.

"I broke things off a while ago, but she doesn't seem ready to accept."

Karina smiles and shakes her head. She has been working for my parents for as long as I've been alive. She's an intelligent and poise lady, like ma. Probably why they're close.

"You've got to sort out that situation quickly."

"I thought I had."

"Women could never leave you alone. I hope you find the right one, settle down, and bring us some grandkids."

I smile and look down. I've never been fussed about marriage. Now that Karina says she hopes that I meet the right one, my mind wanders to Eve. Initially, I found her intriguing, but now I've developed feelings for her.

"Who is she?" Karina cuts into my thoughts.

"Who did what?" I ask. She narrows her gaze at me.

"The one you're seeing."

"Who said I'm seeing anyone?" I could never hide things from her.

"Henry."

I kiss her on the cheek. "I'll see you later." I leave the kitchen before she can interrogate me further. I take Steph with me, and we leave the house.

"Where are you parked?" I ask her.

"I took the taxi," she says. I guess now I have to take her home. I open the door for her and climbs in cheerfully.

"How did you get the address to my parents' house?"

"I have my ways." She smiles as if she's cute, but I'm not pleased with her antics.

"Please don't ever do that again."

"You weren't replying to my messages."

I sigh. She doesn't understand that I'm no longer interested in her. I don't want to be impolite, but she's forcing my hand.

"That doesn't give you the right to obtain personal information without permission and just show up unannounced. Then tell my family that we're in a relationship."

She looks at me with a look of hurt, but I'm not moved. She brought it upon herself.

"Is there someone else?" she asks. She's so conceited. She can't believe that I simply wouldn't be interested in her. Yes, I was initially into her, but there's nothing more to her than her looks.

"I called things off because there was no future for us. Since then, I have met someone else."

"She's prettier than me?"

"It's not just about looks."

"So, she isn't?"

I ignore her. She doesn't seem to understand that looks aren't everything. Eve is more beautiful than she is and far much more interesting, intelligent, and has manners. Eve has many layers to her, and I want to peel them back one by one. I want to get to the core of who she is. She has her walls up, and I want her to let me in.

I drop Steph off at her parents' house and drive back to mine. I hope that's the last of her I see.

Chapter 19
Eve

I'm sitting at my desk typing something up when Stephanie and Sharon step out of the lift. They're both wearing expensive dresses and duster coats, and high heels. Stephanie has a lot of make-up on and a long weave as usual. Sharon has curly bob and brown lipstick on.

"Hello," I greet them, not that I want to.

"Eve," Sharon stops in front of my desk and stares at me as if trying to figure something out. "I can't place you."

"I doubt that we've met. I'd remember."

She smiles. "We'll wait for my husband in his office." She heads into his office, but Stephanie stays back. I'm wondering what she wants now.

"Have you learnt anything about Henry?" She asks me.

"What?"

"Do you have anything to report to me?"

"I'm not your spy."

She frowns at me. "I met his family yesterday." She flips her weave back. What?! She met his family? How and why?

"Oh." I keep my face and tone neutral. It's not like Henry, and I are in a relationship.

"We had lunch."

"I guess you don't need me to keep tabs on him after all."

She sashays off into her father's office. I'm left suffocating from her expensive perfume mixed with arrogance. I connect my Bluetooth earphones to my phone and decide to listen to Stephanie and Sharon's conversation. I can do that, thanks to the bug I planted.

Since bugging John's office, I haven't gotten any useful information. I decide to listen to Sharon and Stephanie.

"What were you two talking about?" Sharon asks Stephanie.

"Just asking her to keep an eye on Henry," Stephanie replies.

"Why? It's not like she's his assistant."

"I know, but I didn't like that he gave her a lift home. It's my way of letting her know not to even bother making a move on him because he's already taken."

I laugh to myself. She's barking up the wrong tree because I'm not intimidated or threatened by her.

"Is he taken?" Sharon asks.

"I'm working on it."

"Steph, how hard is it to make him yours?"

"It's a bit harder than I thought."

Sharon sighs. "I told you what you to do."

"Mum, I did everything you said, but he's still not budging."

"If you can't make him love you, at least make him want you. You're a woman; you should know how to use your assets to your advantage."

They're disgusting, the pair of them. I'm annoyed by them trying to trap Henry. He's a good man and deserves better than that.

"You need to marry him, Steph. Once you do, you'll be set for life, and he'll be in business with your father for life."

Just then, John steps out of the lift. I take the earphones off and greet him. I give him his messages, and then he heads into his office.

**

To my surprise, Henry is waiting for me outside when I finish work.

"What are you doing here?" I ask.

"Evening to you too." He opens the door for me, and I climb in. The car is filled with his masculine scent. It kind of turns me on, not going to lie.

"What are you doing here?" I ask again as he starts the car engine.

"I wanted to surprise you."

Well, colour me surprised. Fortunately, Sharon and her daughter left earlier because if they see with me Henry, there'll be a crazy fallout.

"I would like to make dinner for you," he says.

"Not Stephanie?"

"What?"

"I heard you guys had a lovely lunch with your family." I'm getting annoyed all over again. Henry groans his response. "That's not the way to my house." I point out.

"We're not going to your house," he says plainly.

"Then where are we going?" I don't remember being asked where I want to go.

"To mine."

"We're going to yours; why?" He did say that he wanted to make me dinner. I want to smack my face into my palm. We stop at the traffic lights, and he looks at me.

"Steph decided to just show up at my parents' house, uninvited. I told her not to do that again. She pissed me off." I search his eyes, and he seems genuine. As if he reads my mind, he goes on to explain further. "There's nothing between her and myself. I'm not into her. I want you, and only you."

He wants me? His words make me blush, and I look away before he notices. He uses his index finger to turn my face to face him.

"Eve, Steph is seeking me out and not the other way. I have told her to stop. I don't want anything to get in the way of us."

I hate that he calls her Steph.

"Us?"

"Yes, us. Woman, stop fighting me at every turn and let me be your man." His tone is authoritative and sexy. The treacherous thing in my chest responds, and suddenly my face feels hot. I'm grateful for the lights turning green as Henry returns his attention to the road and drives off. I'm silent for the rest of the journey. I keep stealing glances at him. No man has ever taken that stance with me; I'm turned on.

We arrive at his house in South Kensington. I shouldn't be surprised that he lives in such a posh area. Henry opens the front door and lets me walk in first. I take my shoes off by the door and then walk down the corridor leading to the living room. The floors are made of expensive hardwood, and the house has high ceilings and expensive furniture. The décor is different shades of grey.

"Shall I take your coat?" Henry asks as he helps me out it. Feels weird having him help undress me. It's just my coat, but still. I keep my face neutral. He disappears with my coat and then returns moments later.

He leads me to the kitchen and pulls out a chair for me. I sit down at the marble top island counter. He puts on an apron and takes out food from the fridge and pots from the cupboards. I'm amused as I watch him; he's actually going to cook for me.

"If I get sick tomorrow, we know who to blame," I joke. His manly laugh fills the room, and he reveals his perfectly straight white teeth.

"I'm a great cook. Karina taught me well." He replies.

"Who's Karina?"

"Our housekeeper. I've known her my entire life; she's like a second mother to me."

Rich people. We never had any housekeepers or whatever. It was just gogo and I doing all the housework.

"How was your day?" he asks me.

"It was fine, yours?"

"All better now."

I give him a small smile. He winks as he begins to marinate the steak. I watch him, wondering why he bothers with me at all. He'd be better suited with a woman that gives him the warmth and love he needs. I don't even know if I'm capable of love.

Henry tells me about his talk with his father. I feel bad for him. It's not a pleasant situation he's found himself in. His father is really a jerk for all of this. If people can't be faithful, they shouldn't get into relationships.

Henry serves me with grilled steak and vegetables when the food is done. There are no carbs on my plate. Why do people hate carbs? I shouldn't even be surprised; he's in great shape and probably eats right to stay in it.

He pours me a glass of red wine and then sits across me. I'm not much of a drinker, but I will have this wine. He watches me as I take the first bite and I am shocked. The steak is well seasoned and cooked just how I like it. It's not underdone, and it's not charred.

"It takes good," I say.

"You sound surprised." He starts eating too.

"I am," I laugh. He keeps his gaze on me as I laugh.

"I like hearing you laugh."

Here he goes being cheesy again. I don't respond. I just carry on eating. I take a sip of my wine, and it doesn't taste too bad.

"Tell me about your last relationship," he says. I look at him with a raised eyebrow.

"Why?"

"Because I find it hard to believe that you're single."

I laugh. Really? He finds it hard to believe. I'm not exactly warm and fuzzy. Even he refers to me as icy. Not many men can handle me or want to.

"It was a long time ago. It was very brief; there's not much to tell."

"Why did it end?"

"I wasn't feminine enough for him."

Henry raises an eyebrow. "What does that even mean?"

I shrug. "I'm not cute and bubbly. I seldom wear makeup and dresses. He wanted the type of woman who'd lean on him and want to be spoiled and stuff."

Henry shakes his head. "I guess he doesn't know a strong and secure woman when he sees one. His loss is my gain."

"Your gain?"

"I fully intend on making you mine and never letting go."

The things he says. I look at my food and say nothing. I don't know what to say. After dinner, he serves chocolate mousse cake and raspberries for dessert. I'm full and satisfied when we're done eating.

"Shall I take you on a house tour?" he asks, taking my hand. I feel a jolt of current rush through me instantly. "You have to know your way around and feel at home here."

I say nothing and just follow his lead, something unfamiliar to me. I don't usually follow.

The dining room is on the right, on the way out of the kitchen. It's furnished with a long table and tufted chairs. A massive chandelier hangs from the ceiling. We head into the elegant yet cosy living room. I notice the bar area with all different kinds of alcohol. We leave the living room and head up the wooden stairs with glass panels.

He shows me the guest bedrooms, bathrooms and his office. Lastly, he shows me his bedroom. There's a king-sized bed with a leather headboard. The colour theme is here is navy and white. It's tidy and well organised. Though it is nice and neat, you can tell it's a man's room.

Henry holds my waist with his hands. "This is it," he says. I nod in response. He has a beautiful home.

"You have a nice home," I Say. He holds my waist with both hands.

"It's lacking a woman's touch."

"Stephanie would do a good job sprucing it up," I joke. But he doesn't laugh. He pulls me closer to him, and our bodies are pressed against each other.

"She's never been here, and she won't be coming over anytime soon. The only woman I need sprucing anything up is you, Eve. I want and need you as my woman."

"Oh," I say quietly. I don't know what to do or say when he says these things.

"Eve, are you hearing me? I'm asking, no, I'm telling you that you are my woman." He searches my eyes as he waits for a response, and all I can do is nod. What happened to the fierce me? Where are my words?

Henry kisses me and instantly respond. The kiss is passionate as if we hadn't seen each other in ages. I feel his manhood against my thigh. I break the kiss and look down at it and then at him.

"I won't do anything you don't want me to," he says. His voice is now lower and raspy.

"I want to," I whisper

Chapter 20
Eve

"Are you sure?" he asks me, and I nod in response. He pulls me back in his arms and kisses me. His hands run down my back and gently squeeze my bottom. He groans as he caresses and squeezes my bottom. He starts kissing my neck and finds that sweet spot, making me close my eyes and throw my head back.

Before I know it, I'm in his arms and being carried to the bed. He lowers me gently and then climbs on top of me. He kisses me as he unbuttons my shirt. Thank the lord, I'm wearing a decent bra today.

Henry cups my breasts and kisses them. I'm lying there with my eyes closed, full of mixed emotions. On one hand, I'm enjoying everything he's doing, and I want to embrace him. On the other, I'm nervous. I'm not very experienced with these kinds of situations.

I tense up as he unzips my trousers. He looks at me. "What's wrong?" he asks.

"Nothing," I say. I'm so awkward it's not even funny.

"Eve, we don't have to." His voice is gentle. I don't deserve him.

"I want to...it's just, I'm nervous."

"What's making you nervous?"

"It's been a while, and I'm not exactly experienced."

He holds my face in his hands and kisses my forehead. He caresses my cheek with his thumb as he searches my eyes.

"I'm not looking for a pornstar." He kisses me, slowly and passionately. He runs his hand down my side. He gets onto his knees. "I'm going to take your trousers off, is that okay?"

I nod. At least I'm shaven today. He kisses my stomach and makes his way to my intimate area. "Can I kiss you here?" he asks.

"Yeah," I whisper. I'm nervous.

He lowers his head, and I gasp when I feel his lips on me. I almost lose it at the introduction of his tongue. This is all new to me. He's gentle but passionate.

He gets up and strips. I watch him take his clothes off. Just as I had suspected, he has an impressive physique. His chest has some hairs on it. There's just the perfect hair to skin ratio. He removes his boxers, revealing his manhood, and it's impressive. I gasp and look away. He chuckles softly as he gets back on top of me.

"Are you sure?" he asks one last time, and I nod in response. He kisses me before he makes his way in. I relax. Maybe it's okay for me to want him, to let him please me.

He's gentle with me and keeps making sure I'm okay. It's never been like this. I've never been touched and loved on like this. I hold onto his arms as he claims my body and takes me to a place I've never been.

I find my toes curling, and my back arching as the tensions build up within me. He kisses my neck and my breasts. As small as they are, he takes his time on each one.

His name escapes my lips as the pleasure claims my mind and body. He groans and goes deeper in response.

**

"Morning," Henry says before kissing my lips.

"Hi," I reply. The memories of last night flood my mind, and I start blushing.

"How did you sleep?"

"Fine," I smile. "What's the time?"

"6.10am."

"I need to go home and get ready for work." I cover myself with the bed sheet as I sit up.

"It's not like I haven't seen them before." I shyly look away. "You can use whatever you need in the bathroom." He kisses my cheek. I take the sheet with me, head to the bathroom, and shut the door behind me. I switch on the shower and wait for it to warm up before getting in.

His shower is quite extensive, and the water pressure is just right. The tiles are made of white marble, and the taps are gold. I hear the door open, and before I can turn around, I feel his body pressed up against my back. He starts kissing my neck and touching my breasts. I tilt my head and close my eyes.

I've never had shower sex in my twenty-nine years of existence. And it's glorious. After the shower, I get dressed in my clothes and do the walk of shame. Becky sips her tea and watches me walk through the front door at 7.15.

"Where did you sleep last night?" she asks.

"I have to get dressed quickly; otherwise, I'll be late," I rush to my room, but she's on my heels.

"You slept at Henry's house?"

"I need to get dressed, Becky."

She turns around to face the fire escape instead of leaving the room. I roll my eyes and strip. I change into a brown shirt and black trousers.

"And why is your hair wet?" She asks.

"Got wet in the shower."

Becky turns and looks at me and screams. "His shower?" She cries out.

"Yeah."

"He's such a good looking man. How was he?"

The question is inappropriate, and I want to ignore her, but her big brown eyes are glued on me.

"He was such gentleman."

"Aww. What else?"

"What do you mean what else?"

"How big is he?"

"I have to go." I grab my bag and rush out. He's massive, but I'm not telling her that.

***

I'm sitting at my desk, going through John's schedule. Becky just messaged about a meeting with Henry. Fortunately, these things take time as both men are busy. I don't intend on allowing them to work with each other. The plan was to get John close to getting a deal with Henry and then sabotaging him. After what he and his wife did to my mother, he doesn't deserve good things.

"I hope you don't have plans tonight," says John as he walks out of his office, putting his jacket on.

"Why?" I look up from my desk.

"You're coming over to mine for dinner."

"John?"

"Let's go."

I grab my stuff and follow John out. On our way to his home, I message Henry and tell him that I have a work thing and can't meet him. We were meant to be having dinner together, and unfortunately, I'm now cancelling. I can't miss the chance to go to John's house. I didn't get to snoop around last time.

Stephanie and Ed share the same look of irritation when I walk in with John. They're sitting on the sofa with their phones in their hands. I wonder if they ever do anything else.

"Why is she here?" Ed asks.

"Don't be rude; she's here for dinner." John's reply is abrupt. John's youngest walks into the room. She wasn't there the last time I was over. Unlike her sister, she has braids and no make-up on. She's wearing a simple t-shirt and a pair of shorts. I can see John's features on her face.

It dawns on me that Stephanie and Ed don't look like John. At least Stephanie looks like her mother. On the other hand, Ed doesn't resemble either one of them. John has a bronze skin tone. Ed and Stephanie are much darker.

"Hi," The youngest greets me.

"Hello," I reply. She eyes me from head to toe.

"I'm Elizabeth."

"Eve."

"You can't be Steph's friend."

"Ew, as if." Stephanie murmurs underneath her breath.

"No, your father's assistant."

"Oh?" she sounds and looks surprised. "You're too pretty to be an assistant."

"Am I?" I smile.

"You're in the wrong business. I can totally see you on the runway in Paris."

I laugh. No one has ever likened me to a model. One of the maids enters the room and announces that dinner is ready. Stephanie and Ed rise from their seats, and we all head to the dining room. Stephanie and Ed sit next to each other, and Elizabeth sits next to me this time. Sharon walks in last with her phone in her hand, looking flustered.

"Evening," I say to her.

"Hello," she responds and sits down at the foot of the table opposite her husband.

We're served some expensive wine alongside our dinner. I wonder if they always drink during their meals or only when they have guests.

"Are you old enough to drink?" I ask Elizabeth.

"Yes, I'm eighteen!" She responds. I smile. I feel like she's different from her siblings for some unknown reason. She's undoubtedly friendlier.

"I'd like to make a toast to Eve." John raises his glass. "You've been a real asset to the company. Because of you, we're about to sign a contract with Henry Kobe. I've wanted to get into business with him for years, and you've made it possible. I also heard back from Brixton Hospital, and they were impressed with you. Here's to more years with you by my side."

"Cheers," I say with a fake smile on my face. If looks could kill, then Ed and Stephanie would've murdered me by now. As we eat, I notice that Sharon is distracted. She's barely engaging in conversation and keeps looking at her phone.

After dinner, Sharon excuses herself and goes to take a call. I excuse myself and say that I need to go to the restroom. I make my way down the corridor, this time alone. I don't have an escort because I've been there before. I'm opening doors, trying to see what's in each room. Reckless, I know, but I must do this. If I'm caught, I just say I'm looking for the restroom.

I finally find John's office. I get in and shut the door, and rush over to the desk. I put the bug underneath the desk and then look through the drawers. In the bottom drawer, I find a picture. I gasp as I pick It up and inspect it. It's a picture of my mother. I'm immediately flooded with emotions, but I can't stay too long. I put the picture back and leg it to the bathroom.

I splash my face with cold water. Why does John have a picture of my mother? After what he did to her, he doesn't have the right to keep anything of hers. I dry my face with one of the clean towels and then exit the bathroom. As I'm about to turn a corner, I hear Sharon's voice.

"Stop calling me," she whispers. I slow down and start listening to her conversation. "What do you want?....What?Are you crazy?....no...please..no."

I stand there wondering who she could be speaking to and what they're talking about. I'm assuming that person is why she was so distracted during dinner.

"Mark, don't be stupid. If John finds out that Steph and Ed aren't his, he'll kill us both," says Sharon. I put my hand over my mouth to stop gasping. Talk about being in the right place at the right time. This juicy information just landed right on my lap without having to do anything.

An evil smile splashes across my face as I have just gotten some ammunition to take down Sharon.

Chapter 21
Henry

"I need to tell you something, but you've got to promise me that you won't do anything stupid," I say to my brother Nate, the loose cannon.

"Sounds ominous." He pours himself some of my whiskey, and I don't complain. I lean against the wall with my hands in my pockets. There's no way sugar coat what I'm about to say.

"Dad has illegitimate child," I spit out the venomous words that have killing me, over the past few weeks.

"What?" Nate raises an eyebrow.

"I went to his office and found him with this youngin who claims to be his son. I would've denied it if they didn't look alike so much."

"You're serious?" Nate's face hardens. Though we look alike, he's got a short temper and is more unpredictable. "Did he cheat on ma?"

"Yes." I feel sick just retelling the story.

"What the fuck?" he shouts. Now I need a drink. I pour myself a glass and down it in one shot.

"His name is Matthew, and he thinks he's owed shares in the company. He came to my office to tell me that he should be the next chairman."

Nate's mirthless laugh tells me that he's contemplating something stupid. "The audacity."

"I know. I had to keep from choking him."

"What stopped you?"

"It's dad's fault for stepping out on ma."

"How old is he?"

"Not sure, but he's older than me."

"How?"

"Dad slept with a maid, claims he was drunk. It was shortly after he and ma had gotten married."

Nate shakes his head. "He couldn't even wait a few years to cheat on her. Does she know?"

"No, and that's why you can't say anything."

"Henry, do you hear yourself?" Nate's hand is literally shaking with anger, and I don't blame him.

"If you want to be the one that breaks her heart before her 60th, then go ahead."

"This is messed up." He bangs his fist on the bar.

"I said to dad that he has to tell her himself. He wants to do it after her birthday."

"I'm going to kill him."

I grab Nate's arm because I know he's serious. Growing up, he'd always been the one with the short temper. Half the fights I got involved in were caused by him. I'd fight some twats just because I had to protect my foolish younger brother.

"At least let ma have a good birthday, and then we'll deal with dad and Matthew," I say. Nate takes a long deep breath.

"Fine." He yanks his arm from me and stalks the exit.

"Don't go screwing someone's daughter!" I call out after him. That's another one of his issues, women. He nearly failed med school because he was too busy sleeping with nurses. He always played around too much.

I take another shot of whiskey, and then I'm out of the door. These days, the house is too big for me. I'd love for Eve to be here, but she works too much. The other day, she cancelled dinner on me because she had some work stuff.

I'm at her doorstep less than thirty minutes later. Eve opens the door for me and looks surprised to see me.

"At this rate, we might have to start charging you rent," she says. I narrow my gaze at her.

"Keep talking so much, and I might just move in," I retort. She laughs and gestures for me to come in. I kiss her forehead and then take my shoes off.

"Hi, Mr Kobe," Becky greets from the sofa.

"Since we're going to be housemates, you might as well call me Henry."

She laughs. "Okay," she says.

"It's a Friday night, and the two of you are just watching telly."

"Yeah, what's wrong with that?"

"You both need to go out more."

"I do go out sometimes. It's your woman who keeps me indoors. She's not social, that one."

Eve rolls her eyes and heads to the bedroom. I laugh and follow behind her. I'm not even surprised at her being a homebody. She doesn't strike me as the going-out-to-clubs type. I shut the door behind me and take my hoody off. I throw myself on the bed.

"Eve, come to your man," I say, making myself comfortable on her bed. She's wearing shorts, and I love the sight of her long legs. Her nutmeg complexion is blemish-free and soft. She climbs onto the bed, rests on her elbow, and looks down at me.

"How are you?" She asks, placing her cold hand on my chest. I gasp and flinch. "What?" her eyes widen.

"Your hands are so cold." A look of embarrassment flashes her face, and she moves her hand away.

"Babe, I'm playing." I'm surprised to see a sensitive side to her. She looks away from me. I wrap my arms around her and kiss her neck. "I'm sorry, don't be mad."

"I'm not mad." I don't believe her, but I don't press further. I take her hands into mine and bring them to my lips. I kiss both her hands.

"I missed you."

"You saw me a few days ago."

"It's not enough. I want to see you every day." I kiss her cheek. I feel her relax in my arms. The last man she was with must have done a number on her; she always has her guard up.

I start singing to her. She always puts up a front, but I know she likes it. I caress her hands as I sing to her. She turns and looks at me with a frown and a smile.

"You're a strange man," she says.

"I'm your strange man." I kiss her soft lips. Our tongues meet, and the kiss becomes more passionate. I had missed her so much. I slide my hand into her t-shirt and caress her soft skin. I make my way up to her breasts. Though her breasts are small, they're sensitive and bring her so much pleasure, and it arouses me so much.

I'm on top of her in no time, and we're both naked. She looks into my eyes and runs her hands down my chest. She's a bit freer today than our first time. I trail kisses on her body.

"You're beautiful," I tell her. My voice is low and raspy with desire. I've never wanted a woman the way I want Eve. She runs her hands through my beard and smiles at me. I gently ease inside of her. I take my time with her and make sure she's comfortable. She lays underneath me, holding onto my arms as I make love to her. The way she screams my name drives me crazy.

"I love you." The three words I've never said to any woman just bubble out of my throat faster than I can stop them.

Chapter 22
Eve

Waking up in Henry's arms gives me a feeling I can't explain. I'm at ease in his arms, and it's almost as if everything is right in the world. Last night he told me that he loved me, and my tongue failed me. I couldn't say it back, not because I didn't feel anything for him but because no man has ever said those words to me. I have never said those words to anyone.

I don't think I even know how to love. There's nothing but ice and hatred in my heart. How can I make space for Henry? Maybe I shouldn't have let my guard down and let him in.

"Like what you see?" His voice is groggy with sleep. Again, he's caught me staring at him.

"Yeah." I caress his face with the back of my hand. He's so gorgeous, and he makes me happy.

"Let me take you out for breakfast."

My first thought is to say no, but he told me to stop fighting him and let him be my man. I guess being taken out comes with being his woman.

We take a shower together but no funny business today. There's no way I'm having sex in the same bathroom Becky showers in. I check on Becky before Henry, and I leave.

"I'm going out for breakfast with Henry," I say to her. She mumbles something incoherent in response. I don't try to understand what she's saying and just leave the room.

We're in Westfield, and it's not yet busy, thankfully. I hate crowds. Henry takes my hand and weaves his fingers between mine. His hazel gaze is on me and I smile in response.

"Eve!" Someone calls my name. I turn my head and see gogo standing before me all dressed up in high waisted pleated lilac trousers and a white camisole. The outfit is completed with a white duster coat. Next to her is an unfamiliar man wearing a white shirt and khaki trousers.

"Gogo?" I'm just as shocked to see her as she is to see me. She eyes up Henry from head to toe.

"Good morning gogo," he greets her. I look at him from the corner of my eye. Why is he calling her gogo?

"Hello, young man."

"We were just about to have breakfast. Would you both like to join us?"

This man, though.

"Yes, actually." Gogo looks at the man next to her, who I'm assuming is Ernest. He nods in agreement. Henry leads the way into the restaurant that him and I went to the last time we were here.

He pulls out my chair as usual, and I take a seat. He sits down next to me. Gogo and Ernest sit opposite us. To say this is weird is an understatement.

"So, you're the young man my Eve has been seeing?" Gogo asks Henry.

"Yes, ma'am." He replies.

"What's your name?"

"Henry."

"I hope you didn't sleepover at her place."

"Gogo!" I hiss.

"At least we finally meet properly because last time you left quickly." Gogo looks at Ernest. "She had the young man climb down a fire escape in the rain," she says to him, and Ernest chuckles.

"How did you know?" My eyes widen. I thought I had gotten away with it.

"I've lived longer than you, my dear."

"Young love," Ernest chimes in and laughs. I glare at him. "I'm Ernest, by the way." He seems like a cheerful man, but it's too much for me right now. Meeting him as my grandmother's boyfriend is too much for me.

"Say hello, Eve! Don't be rude," Gogo instructs.

"Hello," I mumble my greeting.

"Hello, young lady."

The waitress comes to get our orders. Henry and I tell her what we're having. Then I watch gogo ordering for her and Ernest. He watches her with a cheerful grin. I don't know how to feel about this. I've never seen her with a man in my entire life.

"I suppose I should do a proper introduction," Says gogo after the waitress has left. She looks at me. "This is my Ernest, whom I spoke to you about. And this is Eve, my granddaughter."

"Maggie has told me so much about you," Ernest says to me. Hearing him refer to her as Maggie makes me cringe. It's Margaret to you, I want to scream, but I hold my tongue.

"What are your intentions with my grandmother?" I ask him.

"Eve!" Gogo snaps. Ernest holds her hand and tells her it's okay.

"I love her so much. I just want to see her happy."

"And I am happy." Gogo squeezes his hand. He smiles and kisses her hand. I look at Henry, who's smiling at them. I guess I'm the only one feeling awkward here.

"Were you married?" I ask Ernest.

"Yes. I was widowed ten years ago." He speaks so carefully as if thinking about every word.

"Do you have children?"

"Yes, we had a son."

"Has he met my grandmother?"

"He passed on six years ago. Sadly, he didn't have any children." He suddenly looks sad.

"Okay, enough with the questions, Eve," Gogo intervenes. I still had plenty of questions, but they'll have to keep. She directs her attention to Henry. "My Eve has never introduced me to anyone she's ever dated. I was starting to get worried."

Henry smiles. "I'll be the only one she'll ever introduce to you," he says confidently. I raise an eyebrow at him.

"Is that so?" Gogo looks intrigued. Henry holds my hand under the table, and I can't help but smile. I'm starting to get used to his touch.

"Yes, ma'am."

"You love my granddaughter?"

"Gogo!" I yelp. Not this topic again. I already left him hanging when he said it last night. I'm not sure if he said it because he loves me or because he was aroused.

"What's wrong with asking that?"

I'm so grateful that I could kiss the waitress for interrupting. She gives us our food, and we start eating. Gogo asks Henry what he does for a living and about his family. So long as it's not about his feelings for me. I'm quiet as I eat, I don't want to speak to Ernest, and I don't want gogo to say too much to Henry.

"It's amazing how you look like Amara," Gogo says to me randomly.

"Oh?" I don't know what to say.

"Amara?" Henry asks.

"Her mother. Eve looks like her, but they're so different. Amara was soft, bubbly and free-spirited. I don't know how Eve ended up so awkward and uptight." Here gogo goes again, being savage. "Before I die, I just want to see her truly happy and enjoy life. Is she good to you?"

What the heck? Shouldn't she be asking me If Henry is good to me?

Henry kisses my hand. "She's good to me," he replies. I disagree with him. I don't think I'm good to him. He deserves more than I can give him.

After breakfast, Henry pays for everything. I notice gogo's face; she's impressed. She goes off with Ernest, and I'm left wondering where they're going and what they will do.

"What's the matter?" Henry wraps his arm around my waist as we head out of the mall.

"Meeting her boyfriend was so weird," I say.

"Why?"

"It's always been us. There's never been anyone else in her life."

"She seems happy."

I cross my arms over my chest. "As long as he doesn't hurt her, I suppose," I mumble. I feel like a selfish child. I'm a myriad of emotions, and I don't know what to do. Henry stops walking pulls me into his arms. I loosen my arms and rest my head on his chest.

"It's a new and unfamiliar situation. Understandably, you're having a hard time. I'm here if you want to talk. But you have to be there for gogo and be happy for her. She's lived for you, and now she's living for herself." He kisses me on my forehead and rubs my back. I'm suddenly feeling emotional. I don't know if it's because of gogo's relationship or the feeling of being in Henry's arms like this scares me.

Chapter 23
Henry

I'm leaning against my car when Eve steps out of the building. She's always beautiful, but today she's beyond that. The yellow high neck dress with a scooped back she's wearing fits her like a glove. I have never seen her in bright colours, and my God, I was missing out. The dress has a slit on the side, revealing her beautiful legs. Her hair is styled in S-waves, and she's wearing just a little bit of make-up.

"What, do I look bad?" she asks as she approaches. I shake my head. As if she could ever look bad.

"You're gorgeous." I kiss her hand and then her lips. I feel a jolt in my groin. It's going to be hard trying to be around her all night. I just want to take her back upstairs and move love to her until morning.

"Are you sure? I don't want to look inappropriate in front of your parents."

"Don't worry, you won't." I open the door for her, and she gets in the car. I slowly walk around the car, trying to walk my arousal off. I get in the car, reach for the glove box, and retrieve a velvet box. I give it to Eve.

"What is it?"

"Open it."

She gasps when she sees the diamond earrings inside. It's not much, but I wanted to buy her something. I want to spoil her and treat her like the queen she is.

"I can't accept them; it's too much," she says.

"Nothing is too much for you, my ice-queen."

Her face is filled with all kinds of emotions. I guess this is something she's not used to. She has the same look as when I told her I loved her. It was my first time ever saying those words to a woman, and I got nothing in return. At this point, I shouldn't be surprised. It takes Eve a while to warm to anyone, and I should be patient with her.

"Please wear them. Let me treat you to things, spoil you and bring the world to your feet. Eve, let me do this for you." I almost plead with her. She can be so hard-headed at times.

"Okay." She puts them on and looks in the mirror. "They're beautiful."

"Next to you, they pale in comparison."

She leans over and kisses me. This is the first time she's ever kissed me first. I'm frozen for a moment. She rubs my chest.

"You look very handsome," she says. I got a shape-up earlier and trimmed my beard. I'm wearing a navy suit with a silk lined blazer and a black shirt. She kisses me again, but this time it's longer. Her chest is pressed against mine, and I feel my arousal growing. I pull back from her.

"You have to stop kissing me; otherwise, I'll take you in this car right now."

Her eyebrows shoot up. "What?" She laughs and reclines back in her seat. She notices my erection and laughs even harder.

"Don't laugh. This is your fault."

She's still laughing. "Let's go," she says at last.

We arrive at my parents' house just before 7pm. There are a lot of cars parked outside. I open Eve's door, give her my hand, and help her out of the vehicle.

"Ready?" I ask her.

"Nope," her voice is unusually uncertain. My beautiful queen is usually confident.

"Why are you nervous?"

"There are a lot of people here, which means I have to make small talk. I hate small talk, and I don't want your parents to dislike me."

"How can anyone dislike you?" I kiss her lips. "You don't have to talk to anyone you don't want to."

She nods, and then we head into the house. Karina is the first to greet us as we walk in. She's dressed smartly as usual in a black knee dress and low heels. Her hair is assembled perfectly into a sophisticated chignon.

"Karina," I kiss her on the cheek as she approaches. She smiles at me and looks at Eve.

"Hello, young lady," she says to Eve.

"Hello," Eve offers a small smile.

"Karina, this my love, Eve."

"Nice to meet you, Karina," says Eve.

"The pleasure is all mine."

From the corner of my eye, I see Nate approaching. Here comes trouble. Karina touches my arm before she walks off. I know that's not the end of it, she must make sure everything is in order for when my parents arrive. She will find her moment to interrogate Eve.

"Hi," Nate stops right in front of Eve.

"Hi," Eve says back to him.

"I'm the more handsome Kobe." He takes her hand and kisses it. Eve shifts uncomfortably.

"As if." I swipe Nate's hand away.

"Better dressed too." Nate teases. He's wearing a baby pink suit and a crisp white shirt. The first buttons are undone, showing off his silver chain.

"I don't know about that; Henry's got swag." My queen defending me. It dawns on that she's never told me that I have swag. Nate raises his eyebrows.

"Meh, he's alright."

Grace and Faith approach, linking arms. I already know they're about to cause chaos.

"Hi," They greet Eve in unison.

"Hello," Eve replies.

"Are you his date?" Grace asks.

"She's pretty," Faith chimes in.

"She's not the one who came for lunch a few weeks ago."

"He's moved on already?"

"I doubt that he was ever with the other one. Didn't you see how his face dropped when she walked in?" Nate Joins in.

"Enough!" I warn. These little twats I call siblings talk too much and will scare Eve off. It's already been challenging getting her to be my woman. I don't need anything rocking the boat now.

"What's your name?" Grace asks Eve.

"Eve, yours?"

"Grace. You're more beautiful than the other woman who came here last time."

"Thank you."

I wish my sisters came with mute buttons. When they get going, they don't stop, and I just know it will worsen today because I've brought a woman home.

"The other one's vibe was off. I wasn't keen on her," Faith comments. Grace nods and agrees with her. Nate keeps looking at Eve as if he's trying to figure something out. Karina rushes in and shooshes us. We all wait, staring at the front door.

"Surprise!" We all yell as my parents walk through the front door. Ma is wearing a long boat neck white dress with some diamond embellishments. Ma is always over the top; I'm not even surprised.

"Oh my," she puts her hand on her chest and fakes her shock. She glides through the room greeting people with such elegance and grace. My father follows behind her, greeting people and thanking them for attending.

Soft jazz music fills the room. As per ma's request, there is a live jazz band. Only the best for ma. Smartly dressed waiters and waitresses swarm the room with champagne.

I whisk Eve away from my siblings for a moment. "Are you okay?" I ask her.

"Yeah," she smiles.

"I hope my siblings didn't scare you off."

"No."

I kiss her cheek, and I see my parents approaching from the corner of my eye. I stand next to Eve with my hand on the small of her back.

"Ma, dad." I greet them both.

"Hello, my dear," Ma smiles, and I kiss her on the cheek.

"Happy birthday."

She's barely listening to me. Her focus is on Eve.

"This is my love, Eve."

My parents share the same look of shock. They look at Eve, then at me and then back at Eve. I wish my family would look less surprised. Eve must be feeling awkward about it all.

"It's nice to meet you both. Happy birthday Mrs Kobe," says Eve.

"Thank you, Eve."

One of my father's business partners waves me over. I hate to leave Eve alone with my parents, and she notices my dilemma.

"Go," she says softly. I rub her back and look at my parents with a look to say behave. Ma understands because she narrows her gaze at me.

"Dexter," I say as I approach the man with the unfortunate timing. This had better be important.

"Henry." He smiles and shakes my hand.

"This is probably not the best time to discuss work, but can we meet sometime during the week." He seems bothered about something.

"Okay, what is it about?"

"A young man called Matthew approached me at the golf course a few days ago."

What in God's name? Matthew is already making his move. I have underestimated him. I don't even get a chance to respond to Dexter. I see an uninvited guest walking and approaching my parents, who are still speaking to Eve. This is not going to be good. What is she doing here?

Fuck

Chapter 24
Eve

Henry has gone to speak to some older man, and I'm left speaking with his parents. His mother is dressed ever so elegantly in her expensive white ball gown. Her hair is pinned up, leaving her honey-coloured skin on full display. She has gorgeous hazel eyes, just like my man. He has his mother's eyes but his father's tall stature and skin complexion.

"Thank you for coming," Mrs Kobe says to me. I'm not easily intimidated, but this woman's aura is formidable.

"It's nice to meet you. I've heard so much about you, both." I say to them. I hope that Henry comes back quickly before I say something awkward. I'm not good with situations like this.

"Have you?"

I nod. "Henry speaks highly of the both of you." Well, until he found out about his father's transgression. I don't dare mention that.

Oh, hell no! What is she doing here?

Tall, curvy and beautiful dark skin. She knows she's gorgeous and walks with her head held up high. She sashays over to us in her long off-the-shoulder red dress with a high slit. She's holding a wrapped box which she offloads to Karina.

"Happy birthday, ma," she says to Mrs Kobe before kissing her on both cheeks. "Evening, father." She says to Mr Kobe. I'm standing here feeling so awkward and angry. Why is she here? I'm sure Henry didn't invite her. I see him making a beeline for me.

"Eve?" Stephanie frowns. Probably surprised to see me there without her father. Henry stands by my side. "Honey," She tries to hug him, but he steps back.

"What are you doing here?" he asks her. His voice is low, and he looks unimpressed.

"It's your mum's birthday." She says it as if he just asked a painfully obvious question. Henry sighs heavily.

"I don't want to make a scene, but Steph, I told you to never drop by unannounced ever again."

"As your woman-

He cuts her off. "Eve is my woman, and your actions are disrespectful towards her."

Stephanie looks at me in disbelief. Not exactly how I wanted her to find out. I don't even know if I wanted her to find out. She eyes me from head to toe, and before I know it, I feel a smack across my face. The room is filled with gasps, and I so badly want to kick her ass but not in front of Henry's parents.

"Stephanie!" Henry barks. At least he's calling Stephanie! He stands between us; he looks so angry. I have never seen him like that. He's always smiling and playful. I gently push him aside.

"You better watch yourself," I warn her. She doesn't know me. I will beat her as if she was a thief.

"How dare you?"

"You want to do this here?"

"After stealing my man, you want to act all high and mighty?"

"First of all, I didn't steal anyone. You can't steal a grown man. Secondly, you're not together, never was." My fists ball up at my side. I want to punch her so badly.

"Eve, I swear-

"You should go. You've caused enough trouble," Mrs Kobe steps in. Stephanie opens her mouth to speak, but Mrs Kobe glares at her with a look that sends shivers down my spine. Stephanie turns on her heel and stomps out of the room.

The music resumes, and Henry whisks me outside. He puts his hands on my waist and inspects my face.

"I'm fine," I say to him. My ego isn't. I've never allowed anyone to hit me and get away with it. I got involved in a few fights growing up, and I always won.

"I can't believe she did that. What a fucking psycho!" He's raging, and it looks like he needs to be checked on.

"Are you okay?"

"No, I'm so irritated. She needs to know what she did isn't okay. No one puts their hands on my woman and think they can get away with it."

"Thanks, my love," He's been introducing me as his love all night. I guess that's what I am to him, so I call him the same. It's weird how it rolled off my tongue so naturally. "Don't do anything else. I'll deal with her myself."

"Eve,"

I wrap my arms around him and look into his beautiful hazel eyes. He's so gorgeous and kind and sexy. I don't know what I've done to deserve a man like him. He kisses my lips.

"I hope this doesn't jeopardize your job."

I shake my head. "It'll be fine," I say. I don't want him to worry or blame himself. However, part of me thinks Stephanie will try and get her dad to fire me. She's such a spoilt brat.

"If things go south, tell me. If you want to get another job or what to start your own business, anything you want, tell me, and I'll give it to you." He searches my eyes. I see the sincerity in his warm hazel eyes, and it warms my heart.

"I'll be fine."

He sighs and nods. "Well, if John tries to fire you, I won't be going ahead with our contract."

I raise my eyebrows in shock. It's crazy for him to forgo business for my sake. I know John has more to lose than Henry, but I'm still surprised.

"Okay, don't go making any rash decisions now." I rub his chest. He's silent for a moment.

"In a perfect world, what would you want to do?"

"What do you mean?"

"Career-wise. What are your dreams?"

No one has ever bothered to ask me what my dreams are. I guess I've never thought about it either. Well, at least not since I found out about John and my mother.

"I don't know. We should probably get back inside."

He grunts. "I don't really want to. I'd rather stay out here with you or sneak away." He plants a few kisses against my cheek. I can't help but smile in response. He smells so good, and his hard chest feels good against mine. My mind is suddenly flooded with images of his bare chest.

"After the party, we can go back to yours," I offer. He pulls me out of his arms and looks at me.

"You can't take that back."

I laugh and shake my head. Poor guy, the number of times I've changed my mind about things regarding him. It's a miracle he still wants to be with me. He takes my hand, and then we head back into the house.

I'm out of my league here, but I came because Henry asked. Everyone is dressed in designer clothes with expensive watches and shoes. We're served tiny portions of posh food intermittently. I wish I had eaten before attending. There's a live jazz band playing, and these people enjoy it.

Henry pulls me into his arms and starts swaying me. "No, I don't dance," I try to protest, but he holds me tightly.

"You do now," he flashes a mischievous grin. I don't want to dance, I can't dance, and fuck! I've just stepped on his toes. How many times will I embarrass myself in front of this man?

"It's okay," he says to me and kisses me. I guess he could see the embarrassment on my face. I don't do a good job hiding my emotions in front of him anymore. "Follow my lead," he says.

He holds out his palm, and I put my hand in it. He holds the small of my back with the other hand. I put my free hand on his shoulder. He guides me in which direction to go. I slowly get the hang of it. It's a standard ballroom dance, but I have two left feet. He gazes into my eyes as we dance. Our bodies are pressed up against each.

Everyone in the room disappears; it feels like it's just him and me. I feel him poke me in the thigh. I've never had a man desire me as much as he does. Whenever we're close to each other, I feel him hardening.

"I want you so much," he says. As he leans in for a kiss, he pauses and whips his head to the side. "What the fuck?"

"What?" I follow his eyes. A tall man with a small afro dressed in a black suit is greeting his mother. His mother looks at the man with confusion. Henry lets me go and rushes over. I follow him, confused, and hoping for no more drama.

"What are you doing here?" Henry asks him.

"Who's he?" Mrs Kobe asks her son. I don't even know when her husband reached her side.

"You shouldn't have come," Mr Kobe says to the afro-man.

"Who is he?"

"Your step-son." The afro-man smiles. "I'm here to wish you a happy birthday and celebrate with you."

Shit! It's Matthew. The balls on him! To just attend His father's wife's birthday party uninvited. For a posh party, there have been too many gate crashers.

"My what?" Mrs Kobe looks at her husband with a scary look that shakes me in my four-inch heels Becky forced me to wear, open toe and thin straps.

"Esther, I was going to tell you," Mr Kobe stutters. The man that such an imposing stature and stern look has been reduced to this stuttering bundle of nerves. Henry is glaring at Matthew as if he's about to kill him. He was so worried about his mum finding out before her birthday. Now she's finding out in the worst way, on her 60th, in front of guests.

"Tell me what exactly?"

"Matthew is my son."

"You bastard." Henry launches his fist at his jaw. Matthew staggers backwards and balls his fists. I jump in front of Henry.

"Don't even think about it," I warn.

"Move!" He barks at me, but I don't move.

"I think you should leave." I'm overstepping here, but I've got to, for my man's sake. Henry is ready to kill him, and I can't have him do that on his mum's birthday. It's bad enough that Matthew is even here. The guests have grown quiet and are now staring at us. It's safe to say the party is over.

"Who the hell are you anyway?"

I see Nate making a beeline for us. "Is this him?" he shouts and rips his suit jacket off.

"So, you all knew?" Mrs Kobe looks angry but quickly composes herself. "Thank you all for coming. Unfortunately, we will now conclude the evening. Travel safely." She turns on her heel and walks out of the room.

Matthew is standing there looking smug. I have half a mind to let Henry go and beat him as if he were a thief.

"Please calm down," I say to both Nate and Henry. I turn to face Matthew. "Get out." I'm careful not to raise my voice. Can't have the guests hear.

"Don't you dare speak to me like that," he says.

"You've done what you came here to do; now get the fuck out." I glare at him with the sternest look I can give. He backs up and leaves. The guests are still standing around, confused. "Go to your mum," I say to Henry and Nate. They nod and leave the room.

"We're sorry for the abrupt end to the evening. Thank you all for coming. Please travel safely." I'm in my assistant mode now. I've just put on a professional face and will act like nothing happened. I bid the guests farewell as they leave. This is all I can do for Henry. This is what I know how to do.

Chapter 25
Henry

By the time we reach our parents' room, ma is swinging golf clubs. Dad is ducking and running away. This is a site I never thought I'd see.

"Esther, I'm sorry," he apologises, but his words fall on deaf ears.

"I thought you were different," She screams out. The graceful, elegant, formidable queen, my mother, has been reduced to a raging scorned wife. I hate seeing what my father has done to her, and I swear to never do that to anyone.

"I was drunk!"

"That's a lame excuse." Ma's eyes land on me. "You knew?"

"I'm sorry, Ma, I couldn't bring myself to tell you," I can't even bring myself to look at her.

"Unbelievable."

"It wasn't for me to tell you." I look at dad with disappointment and anger. "You should've told her from the start."

"I don't need your judgement," he snaps at me.

"It's my 60th, and your bastard son chose today to tell me of his measly existence."

"Esther-" Before dad can say anything else, ma cuts him off.

"Get out!"

"Let's go," I say to Nate. I know ma was kicking dad out and not us, but I can't stand here any longer witnessing their fight. It's just so wrong. Grace and faith are standing outside, and Grace is crying. I had forgotten about them in all that chaos.

"So, it's true?" Faith asks me. I wish I didn't have to break this news to them.

"Yeah." I wrap my arms around them both. "Go to your rooms and stay there. Let ma and dad sort out their parents, okay?"

"Did he cheat on ma?" Grace asks between sobs. I can't tell her that he did. It'll break her heart, but she will know the truth eventually. "Please go to your room and just stay there. Please?"

Nate is just standing there with his hands in his pockets and shaking his head.

"Okay." Faith takes her hand, and they both walk off. I curse under my breath. Matthew has caused so much damage in such a short time.

"I can't believe dad would do that to ma," Nate says to me as we head back downstairs.

"I'm going to strangle that lanky piece of shit. He thinks he can come here and wreak havoc." I'm fuming. Matthew doesn't know me, but soon, he will.

I get downstairs to find all the guests gone. Eve is cleaning up with the house staff. I stand and watch her in awe. The way she jumped between Matthew and me surprised me. She was like a lioness protecting its cub. I'm too busy gazing at the love of my life that I don't see Karina approaching. She slaps me at the back of my head, bringing me out of my trance.

"Ouch! Why?" I cry out.

"You knew about this Matthew character?" she asks. I sigh, rubbing the back of my head.

"I only just found out." She raises an eyebrow at me, and I know I must tell her the truth if I know what's best for me. Nate tries to sneak off, but she catches him by the ear and pulls him back. "I met him at dad's office by mistake. I couldn't bring myself to tell ma."

"I just found out not too long ago. He told me to wait for dad to tell ma himself," says Nate. Karina shakes her head.

"They'll have to sort it out between themselves tonight, but you're not off the hook," she says. "I understand your dilemma."

"Okay," Nate dashes off.

"I didn't know what to do. Never in a million years would I have thought my father would ever do that. I'm angry at him, and I feel apologetic towards ma."

Karina sighs. "You can never know someone 100%."

I click my tongue. Unfortunately, she's right, and it's scary. "I better go."

"She's the one for you."

"What?"

Karina nods in Eve's direction. "I saw how she dismissed Matthew." Karina and I look at each other.

"I didn't think she had it in her."

"She's beautiful and fierce. After you went upstairs, she politely and tactfully got rid of the guests."

"Really?" I raise an eyebrow. Karina smiles and nods. "Mhmm, goodnight." I walk off and grab Eve's arm.

"There's still stuff to do," she protests.

"There are people for that." I take her hand, and we leave.

We're back at mine, and we go straight upstairs. I take my suit jacket off and chuck it in the washing basket. I start unbuttoning my shirt. Eve wraps her arms around me.

"Are you okay?" Her gentle alto voice is all I need to hear to feel better. I smile and caress her soft face.

"I am now," I answer.

"It's okay if you're not okay. Tonight was a lot for your family." She presses her forehead against mine.

"I just want to be here with you."

"I'm here."

I kiss her lips and carry her to the bed. All night, all I wanted was to be alone with her and make love to her. Now I will do just that. I want her with her every fibre of my being. No woman had ever driven me this crazy. I slide my hand up her thigh, touching her soft skin, making me groan. I know that tonight I won't be as gentle as always. Tonight, there's a beast inside of me, ready to devour her.

Chapter 26
Eve

"Why are you walking funny?" Gogo asks me.

"I'm not walking funny," I frown.

"No, you're walking funny."

I try to walk normally as I bring her a cup of tea. She's watching me, and now I feel so awkward. Henry decided to break me in half last night and this morning. And now I'm walking like a duck. I'm not complaining, though. My legs were shaking uncontrollably even after I reached my climax. It's never been like that before.

"I hope it's not that boy's fault," she says plainly.

"I don't understand what you mean." I know exactly what she means, but I'm not going to admit it. That's not a conversation I want to have with gogo.

"Mhmm." She doesn't believe me. "How is he with you?"

I instantly break into a smile. "He's very kind, patient and protective. He always makes sure I'm okay and never forces me to do anything I'm not comfortable with."

Gogo nods. "I hope you can allow him to love you."

"Huh?"

"You're so closed off; you don't easily warm up to people. It can get tiring for someone to keep trying to get you to loosen up."

I raise my eyebrows and start wondering if Henry is getting tired or if he will get tired. I just don't know how to be anything else other than myself. I hear the letterbox lid slam. I get up and go to the door and pick up the mail. I look through the letters, separating mine from Becky's. I come across one addressed to me from a private lab. I quickly open it.

I smile as I read the contents.

"What's that?" Gogo asks. She's never known privacy. She always wants to know who's calling me, texting me and even about my mail.

"Nothing really." Except it's everything. In my hand, I hold evidence that Stephanie isn't John's daughter. See the annoying young lass sashayed into the office a few days ago. She sat on the edge of my desk drinking a Frappuccino. She left the cup at my desk, and I took that with some of John's DNA. I knew it was a long shot, but I couldn't exactly ask them to open wide while I swab their mouths.

Even if the results are inaccurate, it's enough to plant doubt in John's mind. Sharon will feel the wrath of Eve.

**

I hear the ding of the lifts, and I look up. I don't know why but I'm suddenly on defensive mode. My gut is never wrong; Steph storms out of the lift glaring at me. I get up from my seat; I'm ready for her.

"You bitch!" she shouts at me.

"Watch your mouth," I warn.

"I told you Henry was mine, and you go behind my back and seduce him." Her mother is behind her, glaring at me. If looks could kill. Unlike Sharon, I keep my face neutral.

"I never went behind your back to do anything. That would imply that we're friends or something," I say cooly. Her eyebrows shoot up. "And as far as I know, you and Henry have never been in a relationship."

"I will kill you." Stephanie tries to slap me, but I jerk my head backwards. She better not try me like that.

"Stephanie, get a hold of yourself," Sharon instructs.

"Yeah, Stephanie," I chime in unnecessarily. They both glare at me.

"Was this your plan?"

"My plan?"

"You will pack your things and leave and never come back or contact John." She hands me a cashier's cheque for £100,000. Is she trying to pay me off just to stop seeing Henry?

"A bit extreme, don't you think?" I hand her back her cheque.

"Don't be greedy. I'm not giving you more."

"I'm not asking for more; I don't understand why you'd pay me off to stop seeing Henry. It's ridiculous, don't you think?"

An evil chuckle escapes her mouth. "You think I'm bothered about that. Henry will grow tired of you. A man of his calibre only sleeps with women like you to satisfy his curiosity. He'll soon grow bored and move on."

"Then why are you paying me off? Surely you understand that If I quit, then the deal with Kobe Healthcare will be off, and you need that deal."

"We can manage without you. You're not that special."

"You didn't manage without me. For years you chased them and never got a meeting. I did that within a week."

She looks offended, but I don't care. Stephanie is just standing there with her arms over her chest, watching the exchange.

"Unlike you, my husband didn't spread his legs for a deal."

"Neither did I."

"Yeah, right."

"You're just mad I achieved what Stephanie couldn't." They both look at me in confusion. "You tried pimping her out to Henry, but she failed."

"You bitch!" Stephanie cries out in outrage. I don't react; I just smile at her instead.

"You're foolish, just like your mother. But unlike her, you have balls," says Sharon. My face hardens, and I immediately feel sick.

"My mother?" My fists ball up at my side. There's no way she knows.

"I knew you looked familiar, and there was something off about you. So, I did some digging." She offers a sickly smile. "Eve Chari."

This can't be happening! I underestimated them. They're rich; of course, they can dig into my life if they want to. They have more resources than I do. Changing my name wasn't enough. I knew I'd eventually get caught; I just needed it to be after I had ruined them. I was meant cause them financial ruin.

"You will leave, and you won't say anything to John," Sharon gloats as if she's won.

"I think I'll stick around. John might want to know that he's not the father of his eldest children."

I watch Sharon's face drop. The smug look is replaced with shock and fear. Stephanie whips her head in her mum's direction.

"What is she talking about?" she asks. Pride and victory wash over me as I sit back in my seat.

"Oh, my beautiful ladies are here," John says as he walks out of his office. Sharon is startled, and her hands start shaking.

"Hi Honey," Sharon's voice is shaky.

"Let me take you all for lunch, you too, Eve."

I don't know why John is in such a good mood, but I'll pass. "I have some stuff to do, you go ahead."

Sharon looks at me before she walks off with John and Stephanie. Judging by Sharon's nervousness, I can count on her not telling John who I am. However, that's now an issue for me. Now that I'm exposed, Sharon's knowing makes my plan difficult.

**

I'm washing the dishes when Henry comes over. I ask him to wait for me in my room while I finish up in the kitchen. I find myself cleaning up quickly. I just want to be finished and be with Henry.

I rush into my bedroom when I'm done. "Hey," I say with a smile as I kick the door shut. He's by the dressing table with his hand in his pockets.

Oh shit. Maybe he didn't see anything.

"Eve," he looks up to me. "Whose DNA test are you doing?"

Damnit. He saw.

Chapter 27
Henry

"Are you snooping?" She asks me.

"Of course not; I was trying to leave a surprise for you." I point at the small velvet box on her dressing table. Her brown eyes dart over to the box and back to me. This might be the first time I've seen her nervous.

"It's nothing, don't worry about it."

"Eve, it's not nothing."

She walks over to the dresser and takes the papers. I grab her arm; I'm not letting her brush this aside. I need her to talk to me.

"Eve, talk to me," I say softly. I want her to know whatever it is about; I won't judge her. I wish she would trust me with her feelings.

"It's not mine."

Oh, she's a lousy liar. I raise an eyebrow. "Don't lie to me."

"It can't be mine; you know my parents died." She looks at me with such a stern look. I don't know what she's trying to hide from me.

"Okay, then who's ist?"

"Leave it alone."

"Eve, do you love me?"

"What?"

"Do you love me?"

"Why..why are you asking me that?" The sternness dissolves into disconcert.

"I told you that I loved you, and you never responded. I gave you time, I waited, but I don't know what to think when I see you keeping secrets from me. Am I not worthy of your secrets and feelings?"

"Henry, it's just a piece of paper."

"Babe, if it is just that, then it should be alright for me to take a look."

"You don't need to worry about it."

I sigh. "You still haven't answered my question."

She looks at me for a moment and says nothing. She turns on her heel and goes to put the documents in the drawer by her nightstand. This conversation wasn't meant to take this route, but here we are. I've just asked her if she loves me, and she can't answer that.

"Eve, what are we actually doing here? Because I love you, and I want to be with you, you somehow push me away just when we're getting close. You don't want to open up to me about anything. Getting you to talk about yourself is like getting blood out of a stone."

"How have I not opened up to you?"

"Is that a serious question?"

"I didn't stutter."

"Wow." I rub my brow.

"You're making a big deal out of nothing."

I stare at her for a moment. She's not budging. I guess whatever secret she's keeping is worth our relationship.

"Maybe, this isn't going to work out," I say.

"No, it's not," her face hardens. She's gone icy again, and I can't tell if it's because she's being defensive or doesn't care about me.

Once again, I am tasting the bitterness of rejection, courtesy of Eve. And I don't know how to digest it. I've laid my feelings out for her, but she doesn't seem interested. I sigh and walk over to her and kiss her on her forehead. I inhale her sweet scent one last time before I leave.

**

I bang on the door until someone answers it. A short woman appearing to be in her late thirties answers the door with a frown on her face.

"Who are you?" She asks me.

"Is your brother here?" I ask her.

"Who wants to know?"

"Letty, who is it?"

I walk past her and head into the house. I'm searching everywhere until I walk into the living room and my eyes land on him.

"What are you doing here?" he springs to his feet. "How did you find me?"

"As if that would be hard."

"Matthew, do you know him?" I hear Letty's voice from behind me.

"You messed with the wrong one." I unbutton the top buttons of my shirt as I approach him. I throw a punch at his jaw, and he staggers backwards. Letty screams. Matthew tries to hit me, but I dodge and punch him a few times in the ribs and then in the face. He falls backwards, and then I pin him down with my left arm as I punch him with my right. He groans like a wounded bear, but I don't stop. He deserves what he's getting.

Letty jumps on my back. I toss her off my back and then get up to my feet.

"You're lucky your sister jumped in." I'm shaking with anger, and my breathing is laboured. I look down at Matthew. He's lying there with a bust lip and a bleeding nose. His sister rushes to his side and cradles his head.

"Why are you doing this?" she asks me. I do feel bad for her. It's not like me to beat a man up in front of a woman, but I was too angry to stop and think. I had a private investigator investigate Matthew. As soon as I got his address, I came over to give him a beat down he deserved. He disrespected my family and me when he ruined ma's birthday party and when he made a claim at Kobe Healthcare.

"He started it, and I will finish it." I lean down and clean my bloodied fists with Matthew's t-shirt. "I'm going to make sure you don't become the chairman of Kobe Healthcare. You don't know me and trust me, you don't want to me."

"I'm calling the police," Letty says between sobs.

"Don't," Matthew whispers. I click my tongue and walk out of their house. Not speaking to Eve or seeing her for the last few days has driven me over the edge. I'm short with everyone, and unluckily for Matthew, he's at the receiving end of my pent-up anger.

Since walking out of Eve's bedroom, she's not called me, nor has she come to see me. I thought we were getting close, and she was warming up to me. I know she enjoyed my touch; the evidence was all over my sheets. How she reacted to Matthew led me to believe that she cared about me and had my back. But she couldn't even tell me how she felt about me. I'm confused and fed up with trying to win her heart. Am I fighting a losing battle? I need her to sort out her feelings and choose if she wants to be with me or not.

**

I take a deep breath as I walk into the lion's den. I haven't been here since ma's 60th. I dare to show up for the Sunday roast, which I'm not sure is still going ahead.

"Henry!" Grace cries out as she runs towards me. I embrace her and rub her head. She hates it, but she's my baby sister. I can't help but rub her head as I did when she was a toddler.

"Gigi, you okay?" I search her teary hazel eyes.

"No," she responds with a pout.

"What happened?"

"It's been hell here."

I sigh. I'm not surprised. Dad messed up, and we're all paying the price for it. I take her hand, and we head for the dining room, but Karina calls us.

"Drawing room," she instructs. We do as we're told, and when we walk in, we find our parents there. They're not sitting next to each other as they typically would. Ma is sitting in the single tufted white chair with gold legs. Dad is standing a few metres from her with his fingers laced together. Faith and Nate join us moments later.

"What's going on?" I ask ma.

"Your father and I have been talking about Matthew." Ma doesn't beat around the bush. "I'm not happy that I wasn't aware of this bastard, and I hate how I found out. I don't like to be the point of ridicule."

"I'm sorry, honey," My father attempts to apologise.

"Don't cut me off." Her abruptness sends shivers down my spine. "We will stay married, in public, but we'll be sleeping in different rooms inside the home. I'm not ready to forgive your father. As for Matthew, he's not touching Kobe Healthcare."

"Hallelujah!" Nate yelps. His sarcastic tone earns him a chilling glare from ma.

"Esther, the boy is blameless. I can't leave him completely empty-handed," says my dad. We all look at him as if he's lost his mind.

"Excuse me?" I say. "If he wasn't an arrogant twat, maybe I could see where you're coming from."

"It's my company."

"That's where you're wrong." My mother, the formidable queen, rises from her seat like a phoenix from ashes. "I invested in your company with my money; I own shares. And it is my son that continued to build the company and ensured growth and success. What has Matthew done for this company? What gives him the right to my family's sweat and tears. Terrence, you will not test me."

Dad's tail immediately goes between his legs, and he becomes mute. I'm mute too. I dare not add or take away from what ma has said. Esther Kobe has spoken, and her word is final.

Chapter 28
Eve

I unlock the door and take my shoes off as I walk into the house. It's warm and smells of good food and love. Why haven't I been here in a while? I walk to the living room, and my eyes land on gogo. I crawl up on the sofa next to her put my head on her lap.

"Eve?" she says. I don't answer. I just lay there and let my tears wet her skirt. "What's wrong?"

I open my mouth to speak, but my tongue betrays me. I feel gogo's soft hand caressing my head, and I cry harder. My whole body is shaking; I can't stop myself. The tears just keep coming. She doesn't say anything. She rubs my back until my crying quietens. I stick my thumb in my mouth and just lay on gogo's things. She is my haven, my comfort.

"What's the matter, my dear?" she asks gently. She's never me cry like this. I've never seen myself like this. Nothing has ever made me cry like this. It takes me a while before I find my voice again.

"Why is my life like this?" I ask her. My voice is faint.

"Like what?"

"I managed to push Henry away. You warned me. You knew that I was this messed up and hopeless."

"You're not hopeless."

"He asked me if I loved him, and I couldn't answer him."

"And do you?"

"How would I know if I love him?" I've never been in love. I wouldn't know what love is, even if it hit me in the face.

"How do you feel when you're with him?"

I roll onto my back and look at gogo. "I feel like I don't deserve him."

"Why?"

"He's the one that makes an effort to see me. He calls me first messages me. He picks me up from work and takes me out. He's caring and makes sure I'm okay."

"He sounds like a good man."

"He is." I'm tearing up again. "Despite all that he's going through, he still prioritises me."

"What's he going through?" Gogo suddenly sounds concerned.

"Family drama." I'm such a terrible person. I need to be there for him throughout all these issues with Matthew. "I want to be there for him. I hate what's going on, and I hate that there's nothing I can do for him."

"You love him," Gogo says softly.

"How can you tell?" I question her.

"For such a smart girl, you're so oblivious. Get up!"

"Gogo?"

"Get up, get up."

Bruh, she can only be soft for a short time. She's back to her savage self. I sit up, and now here comes Ernest with teas. He gives one to Gogo and the other one to me. I prefer coffee, though. Why is he even here? I hope he doesn't live here.

"It'll make you feel better," he says with a smile. I ignore him. He sits down at the sofas.

"It's so obvious that you love this man. I told you before, you don't bother with anyone or anything you're not interested in. You're here crying your eyes out over him. That's unlike you to cry over anyone. You need to go to him and talk to him."

"And say what?"

"Jesus." Gogo looks at me as if I'm hopeless.

"My dear," Ernest interjects. Why is he interrupting to speak to gogo? I look at him and find him looking at me. Why am I being referred to as *dear?* "Tell him everything that's in your heart. Apologise for the disagreement you had."

"Apologise?" I raise my eyebrows. I already apologised to Becky a while ago. That's my yearly apology quota filled.

"If you care about him, then apologise." Ernest's voice is so soft, it's annoying. Makes it hard to snap at him. "Were you in the wrong?"

I don't answer. I just look down as I'm overcome with guilt. I know the fight was my fault. I wanted to tell Henry the truth, but I was scared. I didn't want to drag him into my mess. I had a plan and wanted to see it through, and nothing would get in my way. Not even Henry with his muscles and gorgeous smile. Not even his warm embrace, kindness and unyielding love.

"My child, talk to the young man. Explain everything to him," Says Ernest.

"Everything?" I look up. I don't know if I can do that.

"What are you willing to hold onto? Him or your secrets?"

Him. I want him.

"If he loves you, and I know he does. I saw it in his eyes every time he looked at you. He will understand, Eve."

I sigh as I put the cup down on the table. Who'd have thought Ernest would have sound advice? He's much softer than gogo. I spring up to my feet and start walking out.

"Where are you going?" gogo shouts to me. I pause in the doorway.

"You both told me to go and speak to him," I reply.

"Okay, go and get your man and never let him go. There aren't too many good ones out there."

I'm standing in front of Henry's house, playing with my fingers. I feel nervous as hell. I never apologise nor explain myself to anyone. I don't know what I'm going to say to him. I take a deep breath and quickly press the doorbell. I have half a mind to run off. I'm losing my nerve. I start walking backwards when the door opens.

I stop breathing when I see him. He's standing before me, in his t-shirt and tracksuit. I just want to be in his arms and hold him tightly. When did this become me? He looks surprised to see me. Someone opened the flood gates because here comes the waterworks again.

"Eve," he rushes to me and holds my shoulders. I'm just standing here, crying like a fool. He pulls me into the house and holds me until I stop crying. I had missed these arms, this chest, this scent and this man. We've been apart for a week, and it feels like it's been longer than that.

He takes my hand and leads me to the living room, and we sit down on the sofa. He wipes my face.

"What's the matter?" he asks me. Where do I even begin?"

"John's my father." I'll just go straight to the point. There's no reason to bury the lead.

"What?"

"John Kasi is my father. That DNA test was to prove Stephanie's not his daughter. I'm such a horrible person. I've not treated you well. I'm sorry. Gogo says I love you."

"Whoa, slow down babe. Start from the beginning."

I take a moment to compose myself.

"John Kasi is my biological father," I Say. Calmer this time.

"How?" Henry is staring at me wide-eyed.

"My mother worked as his secretary years ago. At the time, he was engaged to Sharon, an arranged marriage, but he fell in love with my mother."

"What the hell?"

"Sharon and my father framed my mum for embezzling company funds, and she was locked up. They didn't know she was pregnant with me. So, my mum died giving birth to me in prison. Gogo only told me all this six years ago. Since then, all I wanted was to get revenge on John and Sharon."

"Wow, Eve. You've been carrying all of this by yourself," he says. I raise my eyebrows.

"Huh?"

He pulls me into his arms and rubs my back.

"That's a lot of emotional baggage you've been lugging around. I wish you had told me sooner." His deep voice warms me up. I had missed hearing it. I pull out of his embrace and search his warm hazel eyes.

"I'm not used to trusting people. All my life, all I had was gogo. Then Becky came along, but I couldn't fully open up to her. It's hard for me to trust people with my secrets or my heart. I don't know how to be vulnerable," I explain. I'm actually taking on Ernest's unsolicited advice.

Henry caresses my cheek with his thumb. "I understand," he says. I didn't expect him to understand or care. I've underestimated this man greatly.

"I don't know how to love; I don't know how to be in a relationship. I didn't mean to hurt you."

He nods and kisses my hand. "All I need from you is communication and honesty. I want you to be yourself, but I also need you to let me in."

My eyes are welling up again. Lord, what is this? I don't even get this emotional when I'm on my period. "Okay," My voice is small. Henry kisses my forehead and then my nose.

"Don't cry, babe; I don't like seeing you sad." He wipes my tears and kisses my lips. It's a deep kiss.

I need this.

 I need him.

"I don't deserve you." I look down, but he lifts my chin up with his index finger.

"Don't ever say that. You're an amazing woman, and you deserve the world. What did gogo say about you loving me?"

I look down. "She says if I didn't, I'd never cry like I did."

"You cried to her?"

I nod. He kisses the top of my head and then picks me up, and I wrap my arms around his neck. He takes me upstairs and lays me down on the bed.

Today, he makes love to me differently. It's sensual; it's loving. He gazes into my eyes as he makes love to me. He tells me how beautiful I am and how much he loves me. In such a short time, he's become my everything.

I'll never let this man go.

Chapter 29
Eve

"You finally return then?" Becky asks me as I walk through the door.

"Hi," I reply with a big smile on my face.

"Wow, someone is happy."

I can't deny it. I am happy. I spent the entire weekend with Henry, and we talked a lot. After opening up to him and allowing myself to be vulnerable, I feel lighter. I've never felt like this, and it feels nice.

"Honestly, I wasn't ready to come back." I take my shoes off and head to the kitchen. Becky is on my heels. I know she wants the details of my escapades with Henry. I gulp down a glass of water.

"Aren't you going to spill?" She asks.

"I told him everything about John."

"What?" Becky's eyes almost pop out of their sockets.

"I told him everything, and he was so understanding. I wish I had told him so much sooner, but this is all new to me."

"Wow."

"He doesn't like the idea of me trying to get revenge for my mum, though. He doesn't want me in harm's way, especially with Sharon knowing who I am now."

"What are we going to do about that?"

I shrug. "Honestly, I don't know. I haven't been able to collect anything that I could use against them. I was going to sabotage the deal with Kobe Healthcare, which I don't have to do anymore because Henry doesn't want to proceed after finding out everything."

"You'll give up then?"

"I've got to do something. They can't get away with everything they did to my mum. I can't let them."

"Tell John that Steph and Ed aren't his."

I nod. I might as well; I have nothing to lose. I haven't found any incriminating information. I suspect everything is locked away in his home office, but there's no way of me getting there. The best thing is to share this news with John, let him know that his wife did him dirty for almost thirty years. Besides, I want to let everything go and just move on with Henry. Start afresh.

The doorbell goes off, bringing me out of my thoughts. I go to answer it. I frown.

"What are you doing here?" I ask.

"I wondered if we could talk." Ernest flashes that annoying smile of his. I shrug and let him in. He sits down on the sofa and takes off his herringbone cap. I've never been a fan of those caps; they're so typical for men his age.

"Shall I get you anything?" I ask him, hoping he'd say no.

"Some tea, please."

"How'd you take it?"

"Black."

I nod and head to the kitchen. Becky is looking at me with her eyebrows knitted. "Who's he?" She whispers.

"Ernest."

"Thee Ernest?"

I nod. I get the kettle and fill it up with water. He's lucky I live with Becky; otherwise, there'd be no tea for him. She's the buyer of tea in this house. I sigh as I wait for the kettle to boil.

"I'm going to my room. Fill me in later." With that, Becky leaves the kitchen. I hear her say hello to Ernest on her way.

I re-join Ernest in the living room a few minutes later. He thanks me as I give him his tea. He takes a few sips before saying anything. I'm getting impatient. I want to know why he's here without gogo.

"How did you even know where I live?" I ask him.

"Maggie has an address book." He offers a smile, but he seems a bit off today.

"How are things with that young man?"

I can't help but break into a smile. I don't reply to Ernest's question, and he doesn't press further. He just smiles and nods.

"I'm proud of you. Too many people let pride get in the way of love," he says. Why is he proud of me, though? Hearing that makes me uncomfortable. That statement is reserved for gogo and Henry.

"Why are you here, Ernest?" I'm too impatient. He hesitates for a moment.

"I would like to ask for your permission to marry Maggie."

"What?" I spit out.

"I love her, Eve. We're in our twilight years. I don't want to waste any more time away from her. I never thought I'd find love ever again, and then I met her at the bake sale. She makes me happy, and I'd like to think that I make her happy too."

I'm staring at him in disbelief. "Have you proposed yet?"

"No. I wanted your permission first."

"Oh." I'm surprised. He looks at me teary-eyed, silently pleading with me. I must look like a monster, making an old man cry. "And If I said no?"

"I'd have to respect your wishes."

Shit! Why is he giving me such power? "If you love her, then propose to her. It's not my decision to make."

"But it is my child. You're the most important person in her life. If you're not happy, she's not happy. Besides, by marrying her, we become family too. I'd like to be your family, Eve."

I can almost hear Henry telling me to let gogo be happy. She's lived for me, and now it's time for her to live for herself.

"If she says yes, then I give my blessing. It's her decision to make. I won't stand in your way. If she's happy, then that's all that matters." It'll be weird, though, and it'll take a while to get used to.

"Thank you, my dear. God bless you." Ernest pats the back of my hand and smiles. I return his smile. He can't be so bad if he loves my grandma this much.

**

I take John a cup of tea to his office. Lately, he's been leaving at random times. He doesn't tell me where he's going. Although I'm starting to get curious, I don't care too much if it's nothing to do with work.

"Are you okay?" I ask him. He keeps staring at me, and it's slightly unnerving.

"What was your dream job growing up?" he asks.

"Why?"

"Just wondering. No one grows up wanting to be a personal assistant."

First, it was Henry, and now it's John. I don't think I want to have this conversation with John, though.

"I don't know," I say. He opens his drawer and takes a pill. "Are you sure you're okay?"

"Yes." He nods and takes a sip of his tea. His bald head is shinier than normal. Is he sweating? It's not that warm yet. "You're still young; you can achieve your goals."

"Are you firing me?" Because then I won't hesitate to take the DNA results out of my bag and slam them on his desk. I'd love to disrupt his little happy family with a bit of paternity truth.

"No, never." He smiles, but he looks sad. This is weird.

"Okay." I leave his office, and when I reach my desk, the lift opens, and a smartly dressed middle-aged man walks out. He doesn't look familiar to me.

"Good afternoon, I'm here to see Mr Kasi," he says. He's wearing an expensive suit and is carrying a briefcase.

"Do you have an appointment?" I ask.

"No, I'm his lawyer. He called me in this morning."

"Okay. And what was your name?"

"Colin."

"Please bear with me for a moment." I got into John's office and ask if he wants to see his lawyer. John immediately grants access. I usher the lawyer in and shut the door behind me. I go to my desk and switch on the app so I can listen in on John's meeting. However, I can't hear anything. Panic washes over me. Did John find the bug under his desk?

Chapter 30
Eve

A few months ago, I'd have never gone out on a weeknight, but here I am now, living on the wild side. As soon as I got in from work, I took a shower and then changed into a navy dress. I don't usually have dresses, but Becky and I went shopping for a dress for Mrs Kobe's 60th. She then forced me to buy a few more things because if I'm to date Henry, I should look the part. I thought it was ridiculous at the time, but I'm grateful now.

The dress I'm wearing sits just above my knees, and it moulds my curves nicely. It has thin straps and a very low back. I have to go without a bra, making me feel freaky. I've never thrown caution to the wind like this. I finish my outfit with heel sandals.

Henry gazes at me as I walk out of the building. He's standing by his car watching me. He's looking at me the same way he did when we went to his mum's 60th. I'm starting to feel shy, but I hold his gaze.

"You look beautiful," he says and kisses me.

"Thank you. You look handsome, yourself." I smile. My man's wearing a black turtleneck and black trousers.

"Thank you, babe." He opens the car door for me, and I get in. It dawns on me how easily he uses these words of affection. Maybe, I need to learn to do the same.

We don't go far. We get to the docks, and Henry helps me up the stairs and onto the boat. A man and a woman dressed smartly greet us as we hop on. Henry leads me up the stairs and onto the top deck.

"What's going on?" I ask. A table on the top deck is draped nicely, with cutlery and wine glasses. Henry doesn't say anything and just pulls out the chair for me. I sit down warily. I'm looking around, and I don't see any passengers or other tables. There is a beautiful lounging area resembling a bed with white cushions to my left.

The woman comes with a bottle of wine and pours for us. She smiles and walks off. Henry picks up his glass, and I do the same.

"Here's to us," he says. We clink our glasses. As I take a sip, the boat starts moving.

"We're having dinner on a boat?"

"Yes."

I'm speechless. I've never had dinner in a five-star hotel, never mind on a boat. This is a lot for me.

"Only the best for my baby," he says as if he could hear my thoughts. I smile and nod. Becky told me that I need to learn how to appreciate him and not wonder if I'm deserving or not.

Henry's eyes drop to my chest, and he just stares. "You're not wearing a bra," he says. I laugh.

"No, I'm not."

"What are you trying to do to me?"

I never thought my small boobs would be turn on to anyone, but my man here loves them. He spends so much time kissing them and touching them. The thought of it now is arousing.

"It didn't go with the dress," I shrug. He raises an eyebrow.

"You did that on purpose."

I laugh and shake my head. "So, Ernest came to see me yesterday," I change the subject.

"Breasts, Ernest, yes I see the connection" Sarcasm becomes him. I narrow my gaze at him, and he smiles mischievously.

"He wanted my permission to ask for Maggie's hand in marriage." My body cringes when I say, Maggie. It's just weird, man.

"No way!"

"Yes!"

"That's actually sweet."

I sigh. "I told him it's not my decision. If gogo wants to marry him, then I can't stop them init."

"Yes, but he's being respectful of you. He seems like a good man."

Seems like he is a good man indeed. It's no wonder why gogo is with him. I just want to see her happy.

"I gave him my blessing."

Henry takes my hand and caresses it with his thumb. "I'm proud of you," he smiles. Every time he says that, I feel good about myself. I never want to disappoint him.

We're served with steak and lobster with grilled vegetables. The food looks good, but there aren't any carbs. We enjoy our food as we sail on the Thames. This isn't something I'd have ever seen myself do, but I'm enjoying myself. The city looks beautiful at night. I grew up in London, but I've never seen it like this.

We enjoy chocolate covered strawberries and wine in the lounging area after dinner. We're lying on our backs, looking at the stars talking like old friends. My head is on his chest, and his hand is on my waist. I'm about to do something I've never done.

I put my glass down, and I sit on top of Henry. "Whoa!" He exclaims. I'm surprised too, but I need to show him that I want him as much as he wants me. I lower my torso and kiss his lips.

"Eve," his voice has gone deeper and raspy. When he's aroused, he sounds like that, and it turns me on.

"I love you," I whisper. There, I said it, and I didn't combust. It's not as scary as I thought it would be. He stares at me for a moment, and a smile tugs at his lips.

"I love you too, so much. I've never loved anyone the way I love you."

I kiss him again but for longer this time. His hands find their way under my dress. My phone starts ringing, but I ignore it. I keep kissing Henry, and now I feel his member poking my behind.

My phone keeps on ringing, and it's ruining the mood. I groan and fish it out of my bag. "Let me switch it off," I look at the screen, and there are ten missed calls from John. I frown. Why is he calling so much? The phone starts ringing again.

"Hello?" I answer. Henry frowns at me.

"Ms Gutu?" It doesn't sound like John.

"Yes, who's this?"

"Colin. John is at the Kobe Healthcare Hospital in Knightsbridge, and he wants to see you."

I get up off Henry and stand.

"Is he alright? Why does he want to see me?" It's so late, and he kept calling. It must be urgent.

"He's not well, and he needs to see right now. It must be now."

"Erm, okay." I hang up and look at Henry.

"Is everything okay?" he asks.

"That was John's lawyer. Apparently, John is in the hospital and needs to see me."

"Sounds serious. Let's go. I'll tell the captain to drop us off."

We arrive at the hospital just before 10pm. Henry holds my hand and walks into John's room with me. Colin is sitting on the chair. John is lying there, and he looks so peaceful with his shiny head.

"Eve," he says and smiles. I warily walk to his bedside.

"John? Is everything okay?"

"It is now." He reaches out and takes my hand. I frown and want to recoil, but he holds me tightly. In the past month, far too many people have held my hands. Only Henry is allowed to do that. "I'm sorry."

"Then let go?"

"Not for this. For not recognising you, my child."

Fuck! How did he know? I look at Henry and then back at John.

"What?" I try to play dumb. I'm not admitting to anything! He doesn't have proof.

"Now that I think of it, you have Amara's eyes." His voice isn't loud and bold as it usually is. He sounds gentle and quiet; it's weird. "I met your mother almost thirty years ago. I loved her with everything in me."

"That's not true." I try to snatch my hand back, but damnit John is strong.

"I love her. She was my everything, and I was ready to give up everything for her."

"But you didn't. Let me go."

"I didn't believe that she would embezzle money from the company. A company she helped build. She invested her inheritance in the company."

"She did what?" I spit out. Now I'm raging. These people just used my mum and tossed her aside when they were done.

"I wish I had protected her, but everything happened so fast. I tried looking for her, but her records were sealed, and she just vanished. It's as if someone was keeping me away from her."

"You didn't try hard enough John." What a lame excuse.

"Colin helped me get some of her documents unsealed, and that's when I found out about you. I can't believe my daughter, my firstborn, was in my face all this time." He looks at Henry, who's standing behind me with his fists clenched. "I'm not trying to hurt her."

"Let her go then," he demands, but John is bloody stubborn.

"I love you, girl, and I'm sorry I wasn't the father you needed. Can I ask something of you?"

"Nope!" He must be crazy thinking I'd even entertain doing him any favours.

"I need you to be my successor."

"What?" Henry and I cry out in unison.

"And I need you to look out for Elizabeth. She's still so innocent and needs someone like you in her life." He looks at Henry. "Thank you for loving my girl-

"I'm not your girl!" I cut in.

"Please don't leave her side. You're a good man." He looks at me and smiles. "I'm tired now."

"We'll leave and perhaps reconvene in the morning," says Colin.

"I miss Amara, and I just want to be with her." He lets go of my hand and closes his eyes. I'm frowning at the mention of my mother's name. What does he mean he wants to be with her?

"John?" I call out but no answer. What the fuck? "John?" I shake him. Colin rushes over and starts calling John. Henry comes over and checks for a pulse, and starts CPR. I'm panicking. What's going on? He can't just say all that and.. no. He can't be.

Colin runs to get other medical staff. They rush in and wheel John's bed away. Henry goes with them, and I'm in the room with Colin. I'm freaking going out of my mind. I don't understand what has just happened.

Henry returns after what seems like forever and looks at me sorrowfully. "I'm sorry, babe." He says gently.

"For what?" I'm shaking like a leaf on a windy day.

"He's gone."

** THE END ***

Chapter 1
Nate

I'm running down the lobby with my dick in my hands, trying to not get caught. Yup, I've gotten myself in yet another sticky situation. I stop in front of the lifts and shimmy into my boxers. The doors open before I can get into my trousers, and two women walk out. They eye me up with smiles on their faces. Well, who can blame them? I have a great body, and I'm one handsome son of a gun.

I get in the elevator and change in there while I descend. As the doors open, I dash out and go to my car. I sigh with relief in the comfort of my Bentley. I was too close to getting caught with a married woman, but it wasn't my fault this time. Daphne neglected the truth from me. I was surprised when she said my husband was home.

Henry would be so furious if I got into trouble once again. I've gotten into trouble on too many occasions regarding women, and my older brother has had to intervene. I promised him I would behave, but Daphne was too gorgeous to resist. She is a beautiful woman but not adventurous in bed as I had hoped.

Books in this series:

The Wrath of Eve (1)

The Heart of Sara (2)

Eve's Closure (3)

Other books by Sharmaine. S:

Loving Leah

Switch

Two weeks

For updates on Sharmaine's work follow her on Instagram @herwritinglife

Printed in Great Britain
by Amazon

17314150R00112